The Body Merchants

by

CHARLES NUETZEL

WRITING AS "JOHN DAVIDSON"

The Borgo Press
An Imprint of Wildside Press

MMVII

DEDICATED TO THE TPOH!

SECOND EDITION

Contents

About the *AUTHOR*

Charles Nuetzel was born in San Francisco in 1934, and writes:

"As long as I can remember I wanted to be a writer. It was a dream I never thought would materialize. But with the help of Forrest J Ackerman, who became my agent, I managed to finally make it into print.

"I was lucky enough not only in selling my work to publishers but also ending up packaging books for some of them, and finally becoming a 'publisher' much like those who had bought my first novels. From there it as a simple leap to editing not only a science-fiction anthology, but also a line of SF books for Powell Sci-Fi back in the 1960s. Throughout these active professional years I had the chance to design some covers and do graphic cover layouts for pocket books & magazines."

Much of his work in covers and graphics are a result of having had a father who was a professional commercial artist, and who did a number of covers for sci-fi magazines in the 1950s and later for pocket books—even for some of Mr. Nuetzel's books.

In retirement he has become involved in swing dancing, a long time lover of Big Band jazz. But more interestingly world travels have taken him (and his wife Brigitte) across the world, to Hawaii, Caribbean, Mexico, Kenya, Egypt, Peru, having a lifelong interest in ancient civilizations. His website is full of thousands of pictures taken during these trips.

Introduction

Maybe I shouldn't confess too much about this book. Other than, of course, to admit it was my first novel. But there's a long story that goes with it, for the book originally came out one way, then another that cut some material and added some, and then a third—this version—in which much of the original material was restored. Those alternative editions had more to do with the editorial policy of the particular publishing houses than the author's personal desire. It should underscore the fact that this edition could be called: *the author's cut!*

I've had a chance after so many years to approach the book with a fresh look, and have done much revamping. The story has not changed, but the telling of it has been smoothed out and become the book I wanted it to be, short of starting fresh and writing a totally different novel. But then, I'd have two books instead of one. A somewhat confusing detail that would have forced me to release each under a different title, for each would be, in reality, a different volume.

It was easier, and to me far more desirable, to simply redress this one to suit my fancy.

Hopefully it suits the reader's fancy, too.

It is about a man named Barry and two women by the names of Joan and Ann. Plus a nasty little bugger who owned them all, body and soul. It is also the story of how they found a path out of the tangled mess their lives had become and…well….

They had all taken the easy road to quick money, only to be trapped in the terrible grip of the body merchants. And their freedom would involve *murder*!

And here they are:

5

Barry: who took a job to make fast money, no questions asked—but piloting a hot cargo of call girls proved too much for him, especially when he discovered love in the arms of the wrong woman.

Joan: who was a professional photographer, over-sexed, craving drink and a man's caresses—any man's. She had been sucked in by the good life. Then one night she met Barry, the only man she could ever love.

Ann: the lovely blonde innocent. The image belied her role—mistress of a vicious mobster who needed women as toys and then as products to sell at top dollar as high-priced call-girls.

Blacky: who was tough, heartless. He owned all of them, crushing their lives in his evil, cruel grip.

And on a wild plane ride they would finally clash in a dramatic climax to claim redemption and freedom—at a terrible price!

Well, that kinda sets things up.

—CHARLES NUETZEL
Thousand Oaks, California
August 2006

Chapter *ONE*

Joan Verril's body felt the burning heat of desire; the flesh itself seemed flushed, nakedly tingling to be touched and caressed.

It was one of those hot Southern California summer days that screamed for escape into the arms of some man's embrace; anything, in fact, except facing her oppressive loneliness and physical need.

The air itself seemed to weight down upon her as she slipped off the tight bra, letting her lush, full breasts swing free. Already her body was drenching in sweat that would soon mingle with the man's; a nameless face as far as she was concerned.

"Come on, baby," the male voice rasped.

She moved to him and his hands cupped her breast, fondling her nipples, which grew instantly rigid under the sensual touch.

"You've got...beauties!" he moaned.

He wasn't the best looking bastard she'd given herself to, but the guy knew how to please a woman; he was a good all-nighter.

Then his lips covered hers. She sucked in his tongue, filling her mouth with its moist flesh, thinking how much it was almost like going down on a man.

Her legs parted slightly and she felt the hardness of him. His fingers clawed at her molded fanny.

"You're great, Joanie," the man moaned in her ear.

She sobbed, then clamped her lips around his shoulder, sucking on the flesh.

Joan hated herself this way, but didn't have the will or ability to turn off the passionate fires of her body.

Suddenly she was lifted up in his arms, their lips now

7

fused again in deep tongue kisses. Then they were lying on the bed, his hand between her legs.

"Don't wait!" she moaned, tormented. She tensed, sobbed, moaned as he discovered the depths of her. She couldn't control or stop the fiery desire from turning her into wanton animal, craving a man's body.

When he thrust deep into her, Joan cried out in pleasure and pain. He was rough, almost cruel in his attack.

He thrust again, then again and Joan's hips met each movement with an upward surge.

One of his hands started squeezing her breasts, moving from one to the other, cruel and hard, hurting. But it added to the pleasure.

She felt the sickness that always ripped at her guts when being taken by one of the boys, used like a toy for their sexual hungers. She didn't really want to be so erotically possessed; not deep down inside her real self, but that part of her had no control of the senses which demanded the touch of man's coarse caresses.

Suddenly his thrusting came to a stop and she felt it convulsing in climax. Her own body responded, tensing, experiencing wave after wave of pleasure rip through her every nerve.

The man moaned, lifted away, fell on his back next to her.

Joan still felt the crazed insanity of need and turned, pawing between his legs. She simply couldn't get enough of him. Any man. Once turned on, she found it nearly impossible to turn off, until physically exhausted. And like most men, he responded to her skilled love-making.

Yet the other woman inside her revolted at her uncontrolled passion.

Joan knew she was beautiful and highly desirable; and if anyone should know what was beautiful and desirable to men it was Joan Verril, top cheesecake photographer.

That was a laugh, she thought. *Sex photographer! That was a nice way for a respectable small town girl to end up. But she got good money for her photos.*

With her kind of body it would be possible to have any man; she could have been married, had everything most

8

women share with a special man. But not the ones she now knew. Most of them were pigs, but at least serviced her body, her animal needs. That side of her just loved this kind of wild beast. Blacky Jenson's crowd of hoods considered her hot stuff.

But it wasn't love. It was down and dirty sex, raw, wantonly devouring of body and soul. And with this kind of male animal it lasted until all awareness had fluttered out of existence in the final wave of pleasure.

Some time later consciousness returned. She felt no surprise at the fact the man was gone.

Laying there on her back, naked, now physically and sexually satisfied, the shame returned. Tears started running down her cheeks. Both relief and guilt.

He had come, taken, and then left. Gone like so many others. *How many, now?* She had lost count months ago; maybe years ago.

They had all gone into the night, and once satisfied had gone away. Like this man she seldom saw them leave. She would simply wake up in bed alone and feeling empty and deserted.

She was a deposit for their orgasms; nothing more. The local freebie whore in their eyes.

But, even this honest realization hurt.

Joan longed for someone all her own, who might return to take her into his arms in a tender, loving way. A man who could kiss her with love after having possessed the special gift of her body. And in fact it was a gift. Only thing was that men like this didn't see it that way. To them it was nothing more than a momentary thrill. "Great sex, hot broad!"

But no man loved a tramp; and that's what she was. Yet how she hungered for a lover who was *all* hers.

Like a person that has been flogged, beaten and starved, she moved from the bed, slowly stretching her long, youthful body to its full height, a little under five feet six inches.

She looked at herself in the mirror.

She had a good figure—a damned good one!

Her breasts were full and supple looking; but most of all, they were firm and well-shaped. She had the body that a man wanted and desired—but left once the action was over.

She was a sexual.

One had bluntly told her that, in front of several other couples, at a party. "You give a man a real hard, just look-ing," had been his blunt, crude public statement. Others around had looked embarrassed. She had been furious; though, in another way, thrilled. Later she'd taken the man up to one of the bedrooms; and he'd been damned good. She never knew his name and never met him again.

When it came to a man, Joan was a whore, and knew it.

Joan studied her body, the curve of her hips, and the smooth, flat surface of her stomach. Then she looked at her face, slightly puffed from overdrinking, framed in flaming red hair.

"You're damned good looking. Even if you do drink too much. Still youthful and a man-trap. Why the hell do you throw this body at all and any man...You're over-sexed, Joanie. And you drink too damned much—and that makes you even more needy."

She moaned, still feeling the need for a man and total escape from her thoughts. "You shouldn't drink so damned much!"

But she had good reasons for drinking. With a heavy sigh she moved over to the bar in the corner of the room. It was a well-stocked bar. Scotch, thirty years old. The finest English Gin. All types of Rum. Vermouths, wines, and li-queurs— the best she could afford: and that was the best!

That was one thing she could say about herself; she had a well stocked bar; a well-stacked body; a strong passion for men; a successful business

And she was a drunkard—a lush.

Hate moved through her, rippling the soft, firm muscles of her flat stomach. Her thighs trembled slightly.

Reaching for the Scotch bottle, she poured a strong drink and downed most of it in one tipping of the glass. And shivered from the reaction.

The liquor hit her stomach like a jolt of acid and started working up through her body.

This damn California heat! Or was it something else?

She was warm all over. Her body felt like it was being licked by fiery flames.

10

What was wrong with her? A year ago she had never been bothered like this—or, for that matter, had she ever known what it was like to have a man.

A pure, sweet, innocent virgin!

Things had changed a lot in the past few months. It was funny how much they *could* become so different in such a short period of time. Blacky was partly to blame for that; and his goon-squad served as an easy pool of male bodies to satisfy her sexual needs. Like the man this evening. She used them as much as they used her.

Sitting on the edge of the bed, she took a swallow of the liquor and then lay back full length, looking up at the ceiling.

It was getting worse and worse. More and more men. Every night the same violent need for a caressing body and searching male hands.

She was sick or something. Mentally ill. *No! Not that!*

There was nothing wrong with her mind. It was her body. It cried to be loved.

Stop that, oh...stop it! she cried silently, biting her lower lip, standing.

Gulping the remaining Scotch she returned to the bar. Poured another strong drink and started downing it like water.

Every night was the same; one man after another coming to her apartment. One pawing hand, eager body, naked caress. That was what her life was turning into.

Putting the glass down on the bar, she moved across the room and opened the closet door.

She looked at herself in the mirror. It was a full curving body that faced her in the glass reflection.

A good figure. No wonder the men wanted her! And she sure got her share

Oh, stop...damn you!

Putting on a coat, she walked out of the apartment. She had to do something to kill the rest of the night—anything to keep the burning from tormenting her; anything but drinking herself into a drunken stupor!

The next morning she didn't have a hangover. She never did any more. Just once, she'd like to know she was able to feel the pounding band, playing blaring trumpets in her skull,

11

after a night of drinking and being out with a couple of the boys.

She sighed, as she pulled her car into the parking lot. *More girls, more pictures to take, more assignments to-day...* Parking, she got out and walked around to the back of the building.

"What's new?" she inquired, as she passed her secretary, who was shuffling through correspondence at her desk, in the ante-room.

"A call from Blacky...seemed to think it urgent."

"It's always urgent, Ruthie." She started through the door which led to her private office. "Get him on the phone."

The phone rang. Picking it up, she said: "Hello, Darling."

"Hi, Joan..." Blacky Jenson's voice bellowed over the receiver, with a rasping grate that rocked her ears. "Got a job for you..."

She sighed heavily. A job was all she needed. She was up to her ears with work. "What kind?"

"Have a new boy...at the party, tonight; I want you to show him the normal routine. You know what I want! A Mr. Davis!"

That kind of job! The normal routine...Take him to your apartment, strip for him, then let the sex-starved pig claw all over you.

She felt annoyed, and a stab of guilt. But she was beginning to get used to that. She hated Blacky; hated him for what he had made her into. She hated him more than she did herself.

You're a real bastard! One of these days...so help me...

"Okay, Blacky!" she snapped, wishing she could ram the receiver right through the man's throat. Instead, she just hung up on him, without another word.

Blacky wouldn't care...he didn't care much about such polite formalities. He was only interested in having every-body do what he told them to do —that was all...he didn't really care at all how you went about it, just as long as he got his way.

She felt a cold knot tighten in her at the very thought of what Blacky might do to her or anybody who crossed him.

She knew he wouldn't stop short of murder, if that served his purpose.

The memory of what he had done to his mistress, just because she wanted to leave him, was still too vivid in her mind—that had been horrible!

Chapter *TWO*

It was a wild affair being put on by Blacky Jenson, small-time hood, in the big city.

Several hundred persons had been invited. Barry Davis was one of the newcomers. He was a pilot who owned his own two-bit plane in which he carried passengers, freight and anything else that brought money.

It was Barry's first visit to Blacky Jenson's town. The gangster had contacted him through a mutual friend in New York. There had been a job offer for Barry. Normally he would have turned it down flat, but he was badly in need of money and that was one item that he couldn't do without. That afternoon he had met his new employer for the first time at the big man's downtown office.

They had hardly exchanged the normal greetings when the meeting was brought to a sharp ending.

"You just don't bother about the work none for now," Jenson had commanded in a forceful voice, slamming a huge beefy hand on the tall, sun-tanned pilot's back. "Don't like doing business with a stranger!" he had continued, ushering Barry toward the door of the small business office. "No, I've made it a first rule," his thick eyebrows lifted good-humorously, as he ground his teeth into the thick, black cigar. "See how a man acts at a party, *first!* Then you know better how to handle any possible business affairs. I know a lady who'll keep you company…enjoy her! A fun lady!"

He opened the door then, extended his hand to Barry and bellowed, "Glad you were able to make it, son!" He clapped him on the back once more. "See you at the party tonight. Just be sure to enjoy yourself." His mouth grinned broadly, but his eyes remained icy-cold. "Yes, sir, you can always tell about a man...if he acts right with a woman, he'll act right in

14

any circumstances..."

When Barry walked out of the large office building he shook his head a little dizzily. He'd done jobs for a lot of men before. All kinds. But damn if he'd hit a real odd one this time.

Well, hell! What was he complaining for?

Called half across a continent, all expenses paid in advance, to go to a New Year's party. And a very classy hotel room, as part of the come-on.

Not so bad. Not really bad at all.

Blacky Jenson had his arms around two lovely blondes when they met at the party.

Several drinks had already followed the course of Barry's throat, hitting his stomach like bombs. His head felt enlarged.

It was a wild party. Women everywhere. All sizes, shapes and dimensions.

"Hi there, *flyboy!*" Blacky shouted across the room. "Having a ball?" A gleeful, knowing grin spread on the man's bloated face and his pig eyes twinkled at one of the blondes, as he playfully searched the front of the other girl's dress. With a tired sigh Barry swallowed the rest of his drink, looked around the room and walked toward the bar.

Funny, he thought, *how moods are. When you want girls, you can't have them. They're not around to be had.*

Throw you in a room full of sex-starved, hot feminine merchandise ready to please any male who might ask, and what happens?—you just aren't in. the mood!

Several weeks ago he would have been more than happy to have a pick of such women. He'd been alone, in a cheap hotel room, getting a little high, sexually hungry. So, what had he done? Called for a bellhop. An hour later a plump, mousy-haired woman with a face that might easily have been called horse-like, arrived.

Barry's thoughts were jarred back to the immediate surroundings by a woman pressing against his back.

She said: "Hi, honey!"

Her voice was slurred. But the softness of her large, well-shaped breasts, which had bumped apparently by accident against him, was enough to earn her a second, probing look.

"Oops...sorry," she said, wide-eyed.

He turned, and the woman, who was doing her best to push the both of them off their feet and onto the floor, smiled crookedly up at him.

She was obviously drunk, but the action of her lips had a fully sexual effect on him.

"Sorry..." she mumbled again, as he helped her regain her balance. Somehow he had the feeling she wasn't in the least sorry; and maybe not quite as drunk as she acted.

Her eyes looked carefully up into his, frowning, for a moment. Their green matched the color of the tight fitting dress, which was beautifully displaying her voluptuous figure; it accented the vivid red color of her hair.

All-in-all, this was quite a breath-taking female. He couldn't help responding to her rather blatant sexuality.

Pursing her lips in thought, she reached out a hand and took hold of his arm in the way a woman does when she wants it to be obvious, right-off, that she's not the mere holding-hands type.

"Honey, you don't look happy at all. What's wrong.. . don't you got yourself a girl?"

He looked her over carefully. There was no doubt that this was not the kind of woman a man would be likely to kick out of bed. She was sex, all the way. She made no effort to hide the fact that she wasn't the innocent little girl she'd been born. A slight urge welled through him. It was only an animal reaction.

With a shrug he tried to smile apologetically. "Sorry. Have a girl."

He looked anxiously around the room, his eyes quickly noticing the open doors at the far end which went out to a patio and garden. "Waiting outside for me," he speedily finished.

"Oh," disappointment shaded her face. "I'm sorry. You looked—cute!" She started to stagger away, saw another man standing alone and approached him.

"What you and your girl want?" a voice asked from behind him.

He turned.

16

A bartender was waiting, blank faced. He must have overheard the conversation.

"Oh, that? I..." he started to explain, then caught himself. He couldn't admit he'd turned down a double-barreled offer like that red-head. *It would make him look pretty queer as Hell!*

"Ah...Scotch on the Rocks..." he ordered, suddenly annoyed with himself for *having* turned down the offer; those swaying hips, that tiger-walk—she'd be a real live one! "Two—two of the same!"

The man fixed the drinks and handed them over the bar.

"Thanks." Barry started across the room toward the double doors; he'd have to carry out his farce long enough to make it believable.

Blacky Jenson came flashing by, a brunette at his side, a drink in hand; face flushed; eyes almost blinded with shine. "Havin' shay shwell" was as far as the man got; he seemed to have forgotten what he was going to say or who he was talking to. His hand was caressing the girl's neck-line.

Walking through the open doors, Barry looked around, hoping to find some place to sit. He passed several couples; they didn't notice him.

There was a long flagstone patio which extended several yards out toward the darkness of the large garden beyond. Just at the outer circle of light, reflecting from the house, there was a small table, hidden partly by surrounding shrubbery. He headed for it. Then stopped short a few feet from. his destination.

A young girl, somewhere in her early twenties, was sitting alone. She was looking out toward the garden, her fingers idly working on the edge of an empty glass. She hadn't noticed him.

The girl was pretty. *Very pretty,* he realized.

She wore a red dress. Her hair was silky blonde. Her lips looked velvety; almost child-like—full and red, but delicate. A lock of blonde hair fell on her forehead as she turned slightly in his direction. The light caught in her eyes, revealing a misty, far-away softness; an innocent simplicity. She turned more, her eyes looking straight at him. Actually, straight through him.

She didn't notice him standing there.

"I...didn't know anyone was sitting here," he started to apologize, as those wide eyes finally focused on him. "I was just looking for some place quiet to sit; saw this table, and..."

"It's all right," she whispered absently. He moved to leave.

"Say..." she called, softly.

He turned, paused and took a long look at this misty young woman.

She was beautiful. There was no doubt about it. Her lips were raised up delicately in a friendly smile. "Will you stay? *Please?*" There was a sound in her voice which seemed to be more pleading than suggestive. The whole effect left him a little breathless. She smiled; but her eyes were sad, with a light moistness about them.

"Yes."

She rearranged herself slightly, making room for him next to her. It was a natural action, yet at the same time held some quiet intimacy. For a moment they sat there, not moving, aware of their nearness to each other and relaxing in it, bathing in it. Somehow, he knew she was feeling the same thing. A heady, delicious sense of comfort. If was as if they had known one another for centuries. Like two lost souls connecting. He never believed in soul-mates, yet this was exactly as he would imagine such a meeting between two people may have known one another in a previous life. That was insanity. He simply didn't believe in such stuff. Yet, what he was experiencing at that very moment was something so special that he felt weak and excited, relaxed and tense.

Very strange, he realized. Yet he had heard how people sometimes connected very fast, instinctively.

That was crazy.

Placing the two drinks on the table before him, he looked from them to her. "Have one?"

"Oh...I..."

"Take it! I got stuck with it—didn't want it anyway..."

"I...well, I could use one." She took hold of the glass, running a finger along the rim, looking at it thoughtfully.

18

Then she looked up at him. In that moment he fully realized something very special was happening, and that she felt it too. It seemed as if he were looking right into her soul and it was looking right into his, interlocking with him.

Yet they were total strangers.

You have blue eyes, he thought, *very beautiful blue eyes.* They were sad eyes. Wistful.

"You know Blacky long? I haven't seen you before." She picked up the glass and put it to her hips; sipped it slowly.

"No...I'm new. First party!" he explained, suddenly embarrassed and not knowing why. He avoided her eyes.

"Oh. How you like it?" her voice asked in a very silky, light and resonant way.

"Well, it's—quite a party!" was all he could think of to say.

He noticed her hand as she placed the glass on the table a few inches from his. Her fingers were dainty; long and narrow, ending in red painted nails. He looked at her lips and discovered they were the same shade. *He wanted to kiss them.*

Just like that!

Somehow he knew she would let him, if it were the right time. There was something almost magical taking place between them—some silent bond of sudden understanding which sometimes springs up between people. It was fantastic, but true. He felt that she was aware of it too. It was as if they had known each other for a long time. They met and instantly they seemed to know each other—as if they were on some mental wavelength that connected their minds, emotions and desires.

Sure, she might want to be kissed—and maybe more, but it wasn't the right time or right mood or the right place. She was different from the others at the party. There was an inner class which seemed to demand respect; even though he realized she couldn't really be very innocent about the ways of the world and be here at Blacky Jenson's party. He wondered what connection she might have with the man.

She broke the long silence. "What kind of work do you do?"

"Pilot," he explained, noticing the shape of her dress. The neck-line swooped down only slightly; but it could not hide the form of her delicate figure. "I have a plane which will jockey almost anything, anywhere—for a price. Not much of a life...but—a living."

The low lighting outlined her high cheek bones, and the narrow curve of her nose, as she turned toward the house. For a moment she was silent. Time seemed to freeze, then jolt back into place.

"Why...don't take the job." She abruptly looked at him again. Her expression had changed. The eyes were seriously concerned. "You look like too nice a guy...Don't get mixed up with Blacky!"

He started to say something flippant; but then realized she had meant it. *What could she know about Jenson?*

"Get out, before it's too late!" She looked away embarrassed. After a moment of silence she shook herself, took a drink and said: "I'm sorry...it's none of my damn business! I shouldn't be saying such things. I'm...never mind. Forget all that."

The words seemed strange coming out of such a young, innocent looking girl.

She noticed his surprise. "Don't be fooled by appearance."

"I—"

"No—let me speak!" Her voice was suddenly harsh sounding. She seemed to have made up her mind about something. "I'm sorry. I didn't mean to sound...but, I have to talk to someone. I..." Moisture appeared lightly in her eyes. Her voice was choked a bit; then she gained control of herself. Struggle showed in the tenseness of her body; the concerned frown revealed a maturity he hadn't noticed before.

"I was a pretty girl in a small town..." she broke off. "I don't know why I'm telling you this. Maybe the drinks..."

"No. Go on." He was interested. More than just interested. He wanted to know about her. All about her. "Please..."

"Oh, really it's just the same old story. From rags to riches. From country girl to big city girl. Money, jewels, position, security, when you need it most!" She took a large swallow of her drink. "I tried. I held out a long time. But things got tough. It was after I'd given out to an assistant producer, and been given a few small parts, that I realized I didn't have talent in acting. One thing led to another...and here I am!"

Her eyes fell to the empty glass in her hands, as she finished. "I don't know why I've told you all this. It's silly at hell!"

She looked up at him again. "So, I know what I'm talking about. Once Blacky's got you...you're finished. Trapped; and there's no stopping them..."

Her hands reached out instinctively toward him; hung momentarily in air, and then started back. She looked away; red coloring her cheeks.

He found himself wanting to hold those hands. Feel their warmth; their aliveness; their excitement.

He reached out, taking one slender hand.

It was warm. Soft. And the fingers gripped his; they held him with desperation.

She was looking into his eyes and there was a surprising reflection of his own bewilderment.

He wanted to hold her. To kiss her. To love her. He wanted her more than any girl in the world; wanted to feel her body tenderly held to his. He wanted to know the warmth of her kisses. The soft brush of her hair on his cheek. He desperately needed her.

She seemed closer.

Her lips were very near. They were trembling slightly. Parting.

Then she stood up, turned and ran into the house.

Chapter *THREE*

Barry stood there looking after where the blonde had disappeared, feeling suddenly lost, even desperate. He was shocked at first; then followed her. He ran across the patio and then walked through the crowded room beyond.

He couldn't see her, anywhere. He had to find her! He didn't even know her name.

Going up to the bartender, he asked: "Did you see a blonde in a red dress?" His voice trailed off as he saw the expressionless eyes turn toward him.

"Mister...which one?" the man inquired, pointing to several blondes in red dresses. "Take your pick!"

"But...you'd know her. She's different. I..."

"Yeah, they're all different. Until you get them in bed." The man turned and walked down to the other end of the counter.

Hell!

He searched for almost an hour for her, but she had disappeared.

Several times during his search he noticed the double barreled red-head who earlier had been trying to force her attentions on him. Yet not until he had downed several Scotches did his body really start to begin to respond to the sidelong, encouraging glances she kept sending him. It started slow, then built. It was a familiar feeling. It was an inner ache, burning from his insides outwards. It was desire; animal and sensual.

Maybe it was the drinks. Maybe the blonde girl had started the desire in him. But one thing he knew for sure; it needed satisfying. And the redhead was just the kind of woman who would be easy pickings. She kept giving him quick, meaningful glances, even smiling.

22

The burn and the light airy effects of the Scotch worked their eagerness through his veins.

He needed another drink. He had one; downing it quickly he walked over to where the girl was talking to a hawk-faced man. She had just given him a most direct invitation a few seconds before and he realized that this was as good a time to strike with all his charm and personality.

She noticed him with her eyes again, moving up and down his tall frame, admiringly. Her hips smiled.

"Hey, baby," Barry began, butting into the conversation and looking at the hawk-faced man, who was clumsily working the girl's arm with his fingers. The man's face was violent red, his actions highly nervous. His words were incoherent and slurred.

Barry reached for the girl's arm, taking it from *Hawk-Face.* "You promised me this dance. Remember?"

Her eyes looked eager, but the smile was gone.

"Change your mind, buster?" she stated a bit edgy, yet with a warm intimacy. The words were meant to sting but not crush.

He couldn't care less. If she was willing he'd take her off somewhere and enjoy that lush body.

"Shay..." Hawk-Face grumbled, looking up at him. His eyes seemed to work with difficulty, finding it hard to focus. Then standing he leaned toward Barry. "She's my girl!"

"Sure. Sure she is. But I got this *dance!"*

The man tried to push at Barry; but it was a misdirected effort; a drunken effort that fell to one side of its mark. By stepping back Barry caused the other man to lose his balance and he staggered almost off his feet. Only with concentration was he able to remain standing. Barry helped him fall back into his chair with a forceful shove.

"Come on, baby! He'll forget all about you in a minute." He reached out a hand, pulled the redhead toward him, and smiled warmly. She didn't resist. She moved with a light ease and slid close to him. Her lips didn't smile, but she couldn't keep the interested glow from her eyes.

Hawk-Face stared blankly at them, started to rise, wavered off balance and fell back into the chair again. He grumbled to himself, but was too drunk to do anything else.

23

"He'd not let you get away with this, if he were sober..." she announced, following Barry across the room.

"So, I'm scared silly. See me shake?" he laughed,, then offered generously, "Want a drink?" After all, it wouldn't cost him anything.

This was Blacky's party, Blacky's booze and Blacky's girls.

"Sure thing!" She clutched his arm tightly and suggestively. As they walked he could feel her hips and thighs which occasionally touched his. They were soft. Already he had a hurting hard.

Once they were seated at the bar, he ordered drinks and then turned, looking at the girl. They stared at each other for a long time in silence.

"What's the pitch?" she questioned after awhile.

"What pitch?" he countered blandly, feeling uncomfortable. She was more sober than earlier and he hadn't counted on that.

After all, if you want to make out with a broad, and she's drunk, it doesn't take so much effort.

"No pitch!" he told her after a moment, looking directly at her as honestly as he could. She dropped her eyes to the counter.

"Okay..." she smiled, showing even white teeth behind them.

She really wasn't so bad looking, he realized, *and—hell, what was wrong with him? She was a knock-out! One hell of a knock-out!*

The drinks came. They each downed a good portion.

"What's your name?" he asked, taking hold of her hand. "Mine's Barry."

"Joan Verril." She squeezed his fingers. The action had a seductive quality about it. "You're new..."

"Yeah. New..." He felt like a bug whom everybody wanted to question; all desiring to know what kind of new species he was. "So?"

"So, I haven't seen you around, that's all."

"Well, that's nothing new. I've not seen you around either."

They both laughed at that. He watched the front of her

24

dress move with the sound of her laughing voice.

The drink was beginning to work through him. He was conscious of the warmth of her fingers in his. Their softness.

"I guess you're the new pilot," she observed, taking the rest of her drink in one quick swallow.

"Yes. Want another?" He indicated her empty glass.

She nodded, and he ordered.

Gulping the last of his own, he ordered one for himself, too. He needed it.

There was a dead silence.

The drinks came.

The world was beginning to spin around him by the time he finished this last Scotch. Joan was already weaving slightly on her barstool. He could feel the movement of her thigh as it slipped against his own. *One more drink should do it!*

In the last few minutes of conversation he had discovered her life's story. How she'd come to Hollywood to become a big movie star—and ended as a willing-to-please starlet. *Free lays for the men at the office,* as she had put it.

It seemed that all he was hearing about was stories of rags to riches—casting couches.

Then needing money, she had started taking pictures of girls for the many magazines hungrily begging for them. Her father had been a photographer all his life and she'd worked several summers for him.

"So, you're in the photography business?" he remarked, letting his hand move along her arm. His fingers were aware of the soft fullness of her flesh. It was firm velvet.

She smiled, pressed her leg closer and nodded, sipping some of the Scotch hungrily. Her skin shivered and he felt her press still harder, turning slightly in his direction so that the milky fullness of her neck-line moved into his side. He was aware of the gentle rise and fall of her breathing.

New drinks arrived. They finished them without saying much. Afterwards, when he suggested that they leave, she offered her place as a good destination.

Twenty minutes later they were in a small, modern three room apartment. The drinks were beginning to wear off and she quickly indicated her bar in the corner of the room.

"Help yourself, while I get into something…"

He poured several straight shots of Scotch into two tall glasses, over ice, waited for her return.

It was quite a layout she had, he thought, looking the place over. Modern furnishings; paintings that suggested Paris, London, and other European cities.

He sipped his drink carefully.

It wasn't a long wait.

She came out of her bedroom a few minutes later. A black negligee as wrapped loosely around her body. A white creamy fullness seemed to show through the netting, moving gently with every step.

She smiled; it was a relaxed and pleasing action of satiny red lips. Her eyes were brightly shining and anxious.

After turning down the lights, until the room was filled with only semi-darkness, she stepped over to where he was waiting and immediately slid down next to him.

He could feel the warmth of her as she leaned close. The scent of her was delicate and tantalizing. They sat silently for a long while, just sipping their drinks.

His eyes couldn't keep off her thighs, which were naked and beautiful, soft creamy flesh, perfectly shaped in a voluptuous way. Instinctively, without thought, his hand moved, touched the silken flesh.

Joan murmured. "That feels good."

"You have lovely legs."

She winked. "I hope you think I'm lovely all over."

"I can't wait to find out."

"Help yourself," she offered in a husky voice.

Barry's other hand reached up under the top piece of her negligee, finding the full, lush supple shape of her breast. The nipple was soft, but only for a moment, then responded.

"You better watch out," she warned, "I get terribly hot when a man does that to me!"

"You have exciting breasts," he announced, squeezing the other breast, which was yieldingly full and soft.

"How exciting?" Joan's question.

"You're damned sexy, Joan," he half whispered, his hand again palming her breast. His other hand slipped down between her legs, then under the panties. She stiffened as if

26

hit by an electric shock.

With one hand on her breast, the other exploring between her legs, she returned the caressing with delicate, skilled fingers. It was sexy as hell doing.

God, he thought, *she's got me so hurting hard!*

He became aware of Joan's fingers working with his zipper.

"You're getting *really* hot," Joan announced, her voice thick with pleasure.

Then she squeezed gently, saying: "There's something wonderful about…how that feels."

Joan had said that in such an emotional, though casual way, that the words alone sent a racing electric wave of pleasure through him. Actions blurred, caresses, kisses, all feeding on one another. He wasn't even aware of being stripped.

"Oh, Barry, I just know this is going to be wonderful!" She shifted and suddenly they were touching all over. Their bodies locked in a hungry embrace. The heat of what they were doing was so fiery that it didn't surprise Barry when Joan lifted in greedy hunger against him.

"Oh, Barry, that feels so good…just don't move, don't do anything, yet." Without realizing it, she had engulfed him. Her breasts were crushed to his chest and he was caressing her back, his hands under the negligee. It felt as if she had enveloped his whole being.

Her body was lush and beautiful and alive with erotic passions, yet able to almost absorb an emotional pleasure by just holding him. Her lips mouthed his ear-lobe as her hips made a very tiny circle. Then he heard her moans and sobs of pleasure, then a giggling of delight as their bodies began almost whipping together. At least once he was aware of her whole body going rigid and knew she'd climaxed, but her hips never stopped pumping upon his, thrusting him all the way into her and then almost all the way out, only then to almost drown him in one wave after another of stunning pleasure.

It was almost like a savage dance, beautiful and artistic.

"Oh, *Barry!*" she half screamed, half moaned, as her body almost curled like a coil. She convulsively trembled, tensed against him, and gripped his shaft deeply inside her as if her life depended on it, sobbing in joy as he felt himself being totally drained in an explosive orgasm.

As the ecstasy subsided, their bodies still clutched together, Joan whispered against his ear:

"Oh, you don't know how good that was."

He grinned and caressed her back, tenderly. "I think...I have some idea...you were fantastic!"

She pulled back, looking into his eyes. "Oh, Barry, you were so wonderful."

He laughed, pleased. "What you just did to me was too much."

"Too much for another one?" she teased, lifting up and standing before him.

She reached out and ran her fingertip along his flesh. "I could go on all night with you, Barry!"

There was no doubt about how great her caress had felt, sending little needles of pleasure through him. He grinned and stood, taking her in his arms and tenderly kissing here lips.

Tramp though Joan was, the way she made love was something else. He'd known a lot of whores, but none who had sparked such a response in him. She was so beautiful and so voluptuously knowledgeable about a man; her experience must have been quite extensive. Just the kind of female he needed. Pure, carnal sex with the right amount of tender lustfulness.

No words were needed now. Their desire was already hot and rebuilding. And the honest knowledge of their mutual need caused them to move into the bedroom.

Once on the bed. Joan crushed wildly to him with a violence that revealed the deep power of her own wanting. And in response, his hand moved over her, feeling the full texture of this woman's flesh that was so anxiously seeking his touch. Excited breathing was pounding in his ears.

The negligee slid aside and after a long moment to look at her beauty, he moved against her, more eagerly, more anxiously than the first time. It was fast, cruel, an exchange of wild, erotic kisses and caresses. Then her hips were flush against his, legs parted so that his shaft pressed against her womanhood. A volcanic passion drove him suddenly wild and he was thrust into the depths of her. He couldn't stop himself. His body lashed almost violently against hers, again and again, thrusting his hurting shaft in fast strokes within the grasp of her moist exciting flesh.

Her own responsive actions drove them over the peak so fast that he couldn't believe it.

They exploded together at the same time, then fell away from one another, exhausted, to lay there, side by side for long moments, without speaking.

She was what he had needed. What had been so necessary to get that beautiful blonde innocence out of his mind.

Joan was sex; pure and simple. Nothing else. No questions asked; no answers offered. Direct.

Yet he had never felt such wild excitement, such pleasure, such delightful hunger. And he'd had his share of women in the past. Plenty of them. But Joan was better. She was a clawing cat that moved a man like molten heat.

He looked silently at her; at the shine of her eyes which burned brightly. Tenderly reaching out a hand, he touched hers and all at once knew that the fever, the passion, the fury wasn't burned out yet. Just that touch was all that he needed. It would begin again. It would start at them slowly, grinding its way into their bodies until they would once more find the relief in each other; a relief that was wonderfully overwhelming, ragingly turbulent and satisfying. A satisfaction which demanded and teased and taunted and wanted more of the pleasures, intoxication, and pain-filled ecstasy.

And they began once more, diving headlong into the red pit of passion. By now both of them knew that there was a strong basic attraction between them; a sexual craving drive and compatibility. That was all; but it was all that they needed.

The pit expanded and became bottomless; endless. An abyss that sucked them deeper and deeper into its twisting and whirling depths until exhaustion closed in over their shattered nerves, tired muscles and spinning minds, clothing them in a silken blanket of sleep.

Chapter *FOUR*

The big man frowned through his heavy eyebrows, and then that thick pair of lips spread into a twisting smile. The eyes remained the same; cold; careful; watchful.

"Well, if it isn't lover-boy, pilot-McCoy!" his voice shook through the room. "By George, I was beginning to think you wouldn't take up the bait. If there's something I like, it's a real man...they can be trusted. I understand a man who can enjoy a hot woman. A man with muscles in the right places. And that's just where we're getting. Places. In this business!"

He looked up into Barry's eyes. It was a deep, knife like stare that did more than just question; it dug beyond the outer surface, cutting like a razor.

If there was one man to be careful of, it was Blacky Jenson. That woman he met the night before, who had warned him, might just have been right on. *He'd have to watch him.*

"How'd you like that Verril girl?" the man asked gruffly, leaning back in his seat and beginning to light a thick, black cigar. He sucked a glow into its tip, and then puffed out smoke. "Great lay, isn't she?"

"A girl." Barry shrugged. One of her kind was like all the rest. *A good partner, but that was just about it!*

"*A girl?*" Blacky laughed. "She's *hot stuff.* She's kept around for the boys."

"So...*she was great!*"

"That's better." Blacky leaned forward, looking at him seriously. "Like I said, we keep her around just for kicks, and also to put on the new boys...like you. And she is blunt about rating a guy! You got an A, five stars...and she doesn't joke around about that!"

Barry was beginning to feel uneasy. He accepted the fact that Jenson had been given a report about him from Joan, but didn't like it. Still, apparently that was her job. And there was something he truly liked about her, in a strange way. Maybe it was the blunt honesty; down, basic and not bull. Still it had been a rough night, and the morning had brought spears, knives, vises and steam rollers in, and on his head. Whoever said Scotch didn't give a hangover should be shot!

"Okay," the big man announced in a very solemn and heavy voice. The oil was out of his vocal cords; the muscular smiling of his face had frozen. Everything matched the ice of his eyes. "Let's get to business."

This was it.

Barry felt cold sweat work down his arm-pits. And didn't know why.

Blacky Jenson let silence hold the room for a long time. He let it fall upon his new employee until it seemed a terrible weight. Then his fingers tapped loudly on the desk. It was a booming, explosive sound. It was a rocking jar to Barry's nervous system.

After a moment the man's lips moved. "We have several...ah...jobs that require the necessity of a private plane." He leaned back, and rather airily started sucking on the cigar, his lips wrapped around the end of it, like flexible steel. "We're expanding operations to other cities." Another, louder silence.

"I don't know quite how much you have guessed or picked up, here and there, in conversation about our little...business."

"Nothing to speak of."

"Well, last night's little show was an example, in a small way...*Girls!*"

Barry's face questioned the man.

"Girls. Party girls! You call a certain number, tell when and where you are giving the party, and we supply the sex." He smiled. This time the muscle movement had some humor in it. "Pretty nice racket, I might add. Brings in the gees. Big business concerns will pay a lot—for that, and the other happy things we import to their parties. But that's another matter!"

31

Barry got the message. A dirty racket. Messy. And he didn't know if he wanted to get involved.

"Now that we're expanding to other cities, and want to keep basic operations centered here, it will be necessary at times to jockey some of the girlies to a new destination, in these far-away spots—savvy?"

Barry nodded. *Hell, what was he being so squeamish about? He'd done a few questionable jobs before.* "All I want to know is, just what's in it for me?"

Blacky chuckled. It was a sound from far-north; a chilly vibration in the air. The man's lips quivered, and the fatty flesh around his throat shook. "I like you, flyboy...I like you okay!"

He tried to make himself join his new employer in the jollity, but his lips only made a faint reaction, with only the weakest sound coming out.

He just didn't like this Blacky fellow

"A thousand a trip, plus expenses?' Jenson offered. It wasn't a question, it was a statement, with no monkey-business bickering wanted. Take it or leave it.

The figure staggered him. Damn high. Too high for just flying girls around.

Just for jockeying broods to be made by old men? It was much too expensive.

But, why should he worry? The guy was a nut so why not take advantage of it?

He nodded.

"Good! Good show!"

He took hold of Blacky's hand, and that sealed the bargain.

"Have a job for you tonight."

* * * * * * *

The flyboy had left her apartment early. A call from Blacky had taken him away.

Joan had mixed emotions about Barry. He was terribly nice. Different from the rest of the men that hung around Jenson.

Hell of a lot different! He had been much better!

She thrilled in the memory of how he had taken her so many times that evening. And, strangely enough, Barry had made her feel like a lady; he was the first man to do that in a long, long time.

She remembered how deliciously wonderful the whole thing had been.

Joan realized that this man was the first to ever totally satisfy her sexual cravings.

She paused over that thought, then shrugged. It was enough, Joan told herself, to simply admit she liked him; a lot.

Tall, clean cut looking. Darkly tanned. Strong.

Well built in a lovely muscular way. A dream for any girl.

She sighed. Pulled herself up out of bed. Threw the covers aside and stood. Stretched herself, she felt the blood run through her, bringing an end to the numbness of sleep.

She shivered anxiously, remembering his last words.

"I'll be back, baby—I'll be back—tonight?" Then he had run his fingers along her, softly, caressingly, tenderly—as if he had really meant it.

"Yes...you're good for me!" she murmured, as his lips caressed the soft curve of her throat. Then they had kissed. It was an embrace that left her feeling weak and breathing heavily.

After that, he was suddenly gone. As simple as that. One moment in the thrill-grip of his strong arms, and the next moment, alone.

She dressed, nervously.

It would be a long day. A very long day.

What a hell of a life it was! But, it seemed somehow different this morning. Different than it had for a long time.

Yes, she was right! It was *different.*

It was Barry. That made the difference! She had something to look forward to, besides one aimless session after another; one drink after another; one man after another.

She needed a drink *now,* though. *How she needed one!* It would help to get things moving; rush the day away faster. It would help to bring the evening sooner. And Barry.

Hell, he was just another man!

33

She poured herself a strong shot of Scotch, downing it in one gulp. It hit her stomach. *And nothing!*

Always nothing, she thought bitterly, lifting the bottle to her lips and taking several large swallows.

She numbed.

That was better, her mind thrilled through the slowly binding clamp which was beginning to tighten around her skull. *That was one hell of a lot better.*

Putting the bottle down, she walked across the room, gathered her keys, coat and purse, then went to the door.

She had a busy day ahead of her. Appointment with a producer. Pictures to take of a couple of girls for the magazines; negatives to develop, prints to make.

As she sat behind the driver's seat of her large convertible, she felt happy. She was anxious. Stimulated.

The sun was shining brightly, and it worked down on her skin, soothing it, caressing it, and warming it.

Yes, she thought, *this was just about the best day...best in a long time.*

She could hardly wait until the evening; the evening. And. Barry.

* * * * * * *

Barry had been bothered with mixed and conflicting emotions from the moment he had gotten up that morning, next to the beautiful, seductive Joan Verril.

The confusion had nothing to do with her. Those reactions were easy enough to understand. She had a great body. She was pure passion. And knew how to use both. No questions. No childish demands.

Just get down to business and let it go at that, was her attitude.

That's he way he had always liked women.

Maybe, he realized, *that was why he dug Joan so much.*

She was a hot chick; and knew it.

Yet he felt there was possibly more to her than what she revealed on the surface.

She knew what she wanted and went out and got it. She liked men, and there wasn't a thing she didn't know about the art of making them happy.

She'd keep him sexually satisfied for as long as she was needed for that purpose.

In the meantime…if he could only find that blonde he had been talking to the night before; previous to taking up with Joan.

Sudden, overwhelming emotion twisted his guts in two. It troubled his mind.

He had never felt that way about any other woman. It was more than a sexual urge; it was something far deeper that nagged at him when he thought of the blonde.

Yet, what made her different?

One girl was much the same as another.

But this nameless blonde with the innocent eyes…had touched something very deep within him.

Barry directed the car Blacky Jenson had given him to use while he was in town down the side road which led to his employer's private landing strip. He had things to do on the plane. Had to get it ready. A quick warm-up flight. And there was a lot of work to be done.

His head still ached. Too much thinking! Too much Scotch

This job Blacky had hired him for was a pain. He couldn't help being concerned about it. One thousand smackers just for taking pros up...

There must be something else—something Blacky hadn't let him in on. Something that really paid off. More than just taking call girls around.

But then, maybe he was wrong. He didn't have any real idea how good that racket paid.

Who was he fooling? He just didn't want to be bothered with the idea that maybe Blacky was smuggling dope or carrying on some other—even more dangerous, dirty work.

Blacky Jenson's private pilot, who jockeys girls from town to town to make hay with the local hicks of big business.

What a hell of a job!

Well, he wasn't the one selling the girls. That was Blacky's business—and responsibility. He just drove them to their destination for a nice gee-note.

35

And hell, what difference did it make if he took the job or not? His not taking it wouldn't keep it from being done. Somebody else would just be hired in his place. And he'd be out one hell of a lot of money!

It was take the job, and keep little old Nelly, his plane, or refuse, and lose his money-maker. He was just a little attached to Nelly. Without her, he'd be out of any kind of job. Unless he sold out and went to work for somebody—the last thing he ever wanted to do.

But rotten as the thing was, it had its good side at that, he realized, bringing the car along the narrow, rutted road, swinging it around into a clearing and down to a huge building.

He had Joan, just a-waiting and a-panting to get with the happy-times. Her body raging for any male.

He'd miss her, tonight. He hated to miss a double barreled offer like that...But a job was a job. And that came *first!*

He brought the car to a stop before the large building.

Old Nelly would be waiting for him too. Good old Nelly, and her tarnished, weather worn sides. It seemed a long time since he'd seen her. Only two days. But two days away from his best girl was more than he could take. After all, a man and his real *first* love shouldn't be parted for such a long time.

He jumped out of the car. Studied himself.

He still felt shaky from the hangover. His mouth still was dry. His stomach still a little out of balance. His nerves raw.

The sun hit his face. Blinding him momentarily. Maybe he'd take Nelly up for more than just a test run. It would be good to feel the sky, the air and the floating in space. That timeless, dimensionless area, where nothing else existed except himself and that extension of his mind and hands: *Nelly.*

Sure thing, it would be a gas to take to the skies. Escape from the problems, the emotional agonies—the moral rights and wrongs that plagued a person with every action, every decision they made. Get away from the dirt and filth of earth.

Suddenly something caught his eye. A movement. A figure in the distance.

He jolted. Surprised!

Walking from the hanger building, directly toward him, was the blonde girl who had run out on him the night before.

He could hardly believe his eyes. He could hardly allow himself to admit his good luck. The one person in the world he had wanted to see would have been her.

She hadn't noticed him yet. Wasn't aware he was anywhere near. She was in a world of her own thoughts.

The skirt and blouse she wore showed off the delicate but flowing lines of her figure. She was more beautiful than he had remembered.

Much more beautiful!

He started off in her direction.

"Hello," he smiled.

She looked up. Surprised. Then she smiled, almost nervously. It was a worried and concerned reaction.

A moment later she was standing a few inches before him. And the world had suddenly blossomed into a field of endless bright flowers. It seemed music was playing in the background. That was all illusion. But. Such nice illusion. He was in some cloudy dimension which fluttered with nothing but wonderful things, nameless things, things which just wrapped themselves around his very soul and left him breathless. That quickly shivered as reality set back into place.

And he was looking right into her very soul.

Chapter *FIVE*

"Move a hair to the right," Joan said to the lovely nude model lying on the make-believe beach, in front of a backdrop of netting and rocks. "Just a hair...hold it! Too much. Back! That's right."

The girl was posed so that her breasts stood out rigid and full on her chest, her stomach sucked into nothing, flattening against her spine in an effort to enlarge her bust-line for the camera eye. Her eyes looked at the lens, eagerly awaiting the sound that would tell that the shutter had been snapped and she could at last find relief.

"Just a little bit more, honey," Joan encouraged, wiggling her fingers in the direction she wished the girl to move. "Right. Now, bring out the chest a bit more."

The girl strained.

"Some more."

The globular spheres surged outwards another fraction, vibrating.

"Just a little..."

"I can't!" the girl cried.

"Okay. Hold it." Joan walked around the camera, pointed her light meter at the girl, for a last check. Adjusting the lens-stop, she went back to the camera.

"Say, can't you hurry?" complained the model, in a tight agony.

"Okay, give with the sex...think of a man poking you!"

"Man, hell! Screw men! I'll just think of you, Joanie!" The girl's lips parted, showing even white teeth. "Just you!"

Joan held back a sense of irritation that the reminder that one night she had experienced lesbian relations with this woman. It had been a sick happening; and she didn't plan on having it take place again.

38

"That's great..." Joan announced, clicking the shutter. There was a whishing sound, then she looked through the lens again. "Okay, hon, relax."

The girl seemed to shrivel. Her chest moved inwards, her stomach enlarged, and her breasts seemed smaller, less interesting, less rigid—relaxed.

Joan shuddered in memory of how good it had actually felt to have that woman's body pressed against hers. It wasn't that Joan was any where near being a lesbian; she had been smashed out of her mind, in the woman's apartment, and things just happened.

"Joan," the girl said, "why don't we have a drink together? I'd really dig loving up that body of yours."

"I'm not interested!"

"You were that night. *How* you were interested."

Joan said: "Look, just cut it out. I happened to dig men—not the lesbian scene!"

The other laughed cuttingly. "Those bastards. I can't understand how you..."

"That'll be all!" Joan snapped back nastily. After a moment the other woman shrugged, then stood and walked across the room to the dressing nook in the corner.

"Any more shots?" she asked in a cold sounding voice.

"No...that wraps it up for the afternoon...for you, anyway!" And as far as Joan was concerned, she meant it—in every way. The woman was an annoyance.

Joan was sweating. It felt as if she had been under the bright lights herself. It was a hot day. And she didn't like the woman's blunt offer. But the job had been a direct commission from Joan's publisher. No doubt he was sticking the woman, not knowing about her lesbian kick.

She needed a drink; hadn't had one since that morning. She could really use one, after that woman's blunt offer.

She shook her head against the thoughts, then thought about her coming date.

Lunch with Willy. Cocktails before!

She pulled the exposed negative from the camera.

Sure thing that Willy would want to give her his special cocktail. Wilmore was sure the hell going to have to be in top form, she realized with a grin. But it would cost him in the booze department to have her up his special way; anal sex was not her style, either.

She walked to the door of her darkroom; opened it then stepped into the blackness beyond.

For a moment she automatically considered Wilmore. She vaguely enjoyed his hang-up, anal intercourse, and guessed he probably dug both men and women.

Funny, Joan thought. *It was possible to have fun with a guy who was possibly bisexual, but she found it repulsive to do such things to a woman.* The fact was that a girl didn't have the right sexual tools—even if a dildo had been used on her. It was just that Joan drew a line at how far down she'd go.

At the time when the suggestion of a lesbian relationship had come up, she was drunk, wanting sex and not having a man. Joan had been more curious than anything, especially when the woman showed her a dildo, which looked startlingly real.

She'd asked: "You really use such a thing? Why not dig a man, then?"

The answer was revealing: "Men can't do it right...they are beasts! And they get a girl all knocked-up. I wouldn't let a man stick me for the world; if I could help it. For professional reasons I'll take them on; but really have to fake it. For years my bag has really been girls like you. And I'll promise you one thing, by the time I've worked you over with my lips, in the dark, and started using this big thing, you'll never know the difference."

It had almost been difficult to tell the difference, until climax-time, when there hadn't been the wonderful sensation of a man's shaft convulsively releasing his orgasm deeply inside her.

She shrugged, thinking: *There's nothing wrong in trying anything once.*

The dark-room buzzer sounded and she reached for the phone. "Yes?"

Ruthie, her secretary, said, "Mr. Wilmore is here."

"Okay, tell him to wait. I'll be out as soon as I can."

It was ten minutes before she was able to even think of leaving the darkroom, then another ten before she did. Mr.

40

Wilmore was waiting nervously in her office when she arrived.

"Hello, Willy," she sighed, walking businesslike around her desk. "Just a few seconds and I'll be with you."

"Hello, sweetheart," he grinned. "Take your time."

She would. There really wasn't anything important or pressing she had to do, but she needed a few minutes to gather her nerves together. Pushing several papers around on the top of her desk she tried to act engrossed in important matters. She didn't like Wilmore. He was a crude man; a hard, demanding prick. They'd known each other for some time. She had never found their relationship a very pleasant one—except in a business way. The man was a perverted bastard.

But then, one man was almost as good as another, when it came to business affairs. You let them have your body and then got their accounts. It was simple. Make the boys, and if you are good enough and willing enough to take it the way they handed it out, you got what you wanted.

Business. Contracts. And she could always use work and money.

In show business it was called a "casting couch" but the way she used it, things were reversed. She was in the position of power. If she didn't want their business, she didn't give them free feels.

She looked up at Wilmore. He was dark skinned, naturally—but suntanned. His lips were thick and heavy. His whole frame was thick and heavy. There was a something about the redness of his features that looked unhealthy. He wasn't the out-door type. He wasn't like Barry.

Now, there was a *man* for you.

She felt an anxious warmth at the thought of him, and the coming evening.

"Well, all through," she smiled, standing and walking over to producer Wilmore. "Sorry, I didn't mean to be so long..."

He took her arm and they left the office.

* * * * * * *

"Fancy meeting you here," the blonde-haired girl said to Barry.

They had been standing looking at each other for a long time, in silence. A silence that was heavy with conversation. A conversation that seemed to flow through the air between them. A silence with only their eyes to communicate any feeling, any emotions, any thoughts.

"Well, fancy meeting you..." he smiled back. He was still under the spell of her loveliness. It was a pure, clean loveliness that seemed to overrule the fact that she must be just another of the girls that Blacky Jenson had around. Maybe one he was expected to jockey to some private party this night. That was depressing.

He shivered at the thought.

She seemed the furthest thing from that kind of woman. He found it hard to think of her in that way. Maybe it was the look about her. The appearance of class. *That was it!*

You just couldn't imagine a girl of such fine features, such clear blue eyes, such long simple lines as being anything but pure and clean and good. Her figure seemed to flow with her clothing. With the skirt, the blouse. They seemed a part of her. Normal. Natural. They fit. Thinking of her in the arms of another man was simply ugly.

A pain stabbed through his mind. A raging nausea. A maddening rippling through his muscles. He shook himself. He was acting like a silly school kid. They were both adults; and with adult needs and fighting to survive in a hard world.

"What's wrong?" she asked, her face becoming concerned. Her hand reached out involuntarily toward him, in an expression of wanting to help, of wanting to soothe, of wanting to give.

It froze and withdrew, like it had done the night before.

"Nothing." He felt foolish. What could he say to her? *Baby, I just don't picture you as an easy mark! As a whore.*

Hardly.

"What are you doing out here?" he asked, looking around the country side as if she just didn't belong in such surroundings. It had been a shock, seeing her so unexpectedly.

"I might ask you the same question. I live here."

"You do?" The two words came out of him like blasts of lightning. They exploded on the morning air unnecessarily loud and foolish sounding. He just hadn't been prepared for such an answer. If she had said she was here to see him, he might have found it easier to believe; more pleasant anyway.

So much for self-ego!

"My plane...in the hanger," he explained, pointing toward the huge building from where she had just come. "You must have seen it."

"Yes, how foolish of me. Of course, you said something about that last night. Guess I just forgot." She shrugged her shoulders, as if to say, aren't I silly—*a regular dolt!* The action brought the front of her chest forward, exposing the fullness under her blouse. A surprising fullness, that sparked an urge in him—a tender need, a passionate demand. *God what a joy to make love to such a woman!*

"I was looking at your plane. Quite nice."

"It'll do until something better comes along." Then feeling guilty at that line, foolishly added: "Well, she's a special lady."

"Oh?"

He shrugged, embarrassed. "Okay, call me a nut—"

"Okay. You're a nut," she laughed.

He chuckled added, feeling a bit more relaxed: "I call her Nelly."

"Strange name for a...plane."

"Not really. But, never mind that. She's my friend in need. And sometimes she's needy. She keeps me in business and I have to keep her healthy—and that's sometimes expensive. So...here I am."

"So you haven't changed your mind..." she observed, starting to walk with him toward the hanger.

"About what?"

"Working for Blacky."

"Oh, that. No. Thousand smackers a job is a hell of a lot of money to step out on."

"I guess so."

They continued walking in silence then. Both suddenly caught in their own thoughts. Both wrapped in a shell, a walled-in corner of their own brains. He wanted to say a lot of things. But it wasn't the time—*yet.* Or the place. *Yet!*

"You like to fly? Ever been up?" he asked, when they arrived within sight of his two engine Nelly.

"Never have," her voice quickly replied, as if she had been waiting for him to say something—anything!

Eager.

Anxious.

That was what she was. Eager. Fresh. Anxious.

"Never been up?" Here was his chance. His opportunity. "How about it? I'm taking her up in a few minutes. Like some company?"

She stood quietly for several minutes. Thinking. Concern showed in the pursing of her lips. Worry moved her eyes into a frown.

"Have something else planned?" he asked, stepping closer to her. The smell of light perfume scented the air. It reached his brain centers in a delightful warmth, and dizziness. Looking down at her, so near, it was hard to keep from taking her in his arms. And for some reason he knew she wanted to be held to him, kissed, touched, caressed—but was afraid of something. *Or someone?*

He didn't know.

But magic had taken place the night before. The two of them had communicated to each other as if they had been friends for years. An awareness had built which was stronger than the mere fear which seemed to be drawing them apart.

What fear?

Why had she run out on him? He wanted to ask her. He wanted to know. But he would have to wait. Wait until she offered the information. Willingly and freely.

"No, I don't have anything planned...it's not that..." she whispered thoughtfully, after a long silence.

"Well then, it's settled." He reached for her arm and pulled her along. Her skin was soft, exciting and warm. It sent tingles through him. Sharp points of electric shock.

She seemed to react in the same way. She didn't struggle. She came after him, almost eagerly; glad that the decision had been taken out of her hands.

When they were under the wing of the plane, near the cockpit, something seemed to draw him to a stop. Nothing he

44

could put his finger on, just an impulse. Or maybe it was something in the feel of her. The warmth. The touch of her body as it brushed against his.

He stopped. Turned. Nothing else. No build up.

No questioning. No asking. No fumbling. She had sensed the same emotion. The same thought. The same urge. The same desperate communication which raged between them.

She came into his arms eagerly. Soft. Sliding her hand around his body and up to the back of his neck. He felt the nearness of her yield into a full embrace as her body surged against him angrily. Her mouth pushed up under his, seeking, demanding. The sting of her moist lips, anxious and desperate, was the most overwhelming thing that he had ever experienced. It was more than just sensual. It was explosive. Sweet, passionate. Tender. More wonderful than the animal outlet of the night before with Joan. More sensational, more stimulating, more satisfying and honestly normal.

They held each other for a long time. A long moment that seemed forever and yet at the same time but a brief second. An eternity—that ended.

Parting, they looked at each other. A deep, penetrating stare.

She started to turn, as if to run away.

His hands violently grabbed hold of her. Hard.

"No..." she pleaded, struggling to be free. *"No..."* Her voice was hard, a painful sound. It seemed near an emotional break. It would split wide open any second.

But he didn't care. She wasn't going to get away from him this time. She wasn't disappearing without a word, or explanation.

"No...*please!*" she begged, looking up at him. Moisture was in her eyes. Her face shriveled up in a tormented frown.

"Oh, please!"

He felt defeated. Numb. Helpless. He couldn't deny her anything. He knew that. He couldn't keep her there against her will. He couldn't force her to stay. Not when she looked at him in that way, pleading, begging...

His hands opened and slid along the white smoothness of her arms, then fell to his sides, helplessly.

She stood staring at him for a long time, and then turned and ran off across–the landing strip toward the house several hundred yards away.

Chapter *SIX*

Joan Verril looked at the man sitting with her in the dark, secluded booth of the high-class, expensive restaurant to which she had persuaded him to bring her. She smiled. It was a muscular movement of her lips. She sipped the Martini in her hands, and felt the happy contents liven her stomach. Sipped some more, and was pleased to feel a numbness slide through her. She needed it.

This slob, she realized, would be starting his little: Let's play tootsies under the table.

Almost on cue, she felt his shoe run up her leg, very lightly, then suddenly he was placing his foot on her lap, between her legs, pressing her crotch. She wiggled sensually against the shoe—as was expected of her. Then she lifted her feet, having already kicked off her high-heeled shoes and put her toes against his crotch.

God, she thought, *he's a rock!*

Despite herself, Joan felt a churning sense of excitement as her toes wiggled and explored between his legs, under the table. Nobody but the two of them could know what was going on; but she could tell from the expression on his face that her play was exciting him.

Smiling knowingly at him, she asked: "How do you feel—now?"

His lips spread thin, the obvious pleasure was marked on every line of his face.

"Just like a little kid," she teased, forcing herself to play out the game he liked; for only one reason: she wanted sex, and he could sock it to her. And he was important enough to make an outward effort to please.

She winked, teasingly, then lowered her foot, found her shoe and after a quick struggle got it on. He had already

47

dropped his own foot. The game was over—for the moment! She hated herself for wanting a man so bad that she'd be able to enjoy even this prig.

He said, then: "That's what I like about you you're so cooperative."

The double meaning was obvious enough to Joan; and irritating. Just for kicks she said, nastily: "Well, Willy, you've given me the latest of all the latest at your studio, your worries at home and what else...*new,* what's *new?*"

"It's the same bag of crap! That's why I need a little fun-girl like you!" He looked meaningfully at her neckline.

Joan knew exactly how he'd meant that remark.

It still bugged her. Men like Willy served a purpose; but she didn't like the idea of being considered a whore, to be used and tossed aside after the fun and games had been completed. Even if she was the one in control; she didn't like having them think otherwise.

Life was a dirty trap for a woman like herself; it would have been better if she'd never learned about sex. But that kind of knowledge had come early. One of her "teachers" had been a cousin who just came out and said she was too sexy to not be screwed and he was just the guy to teach her the facts of life. The trouble was that he'd exposed himself so quick that it was impossible to bring a stop to what followed.

Joan sighed, looking at Willy. Even he could be fun to play with.

Still, she couldn't help a sharp dig, just to put him in his blasted place. The least a man should do is "act" respectful to a woman—no matter how much of a whore she might be.

"Why, Willy, dear, one would think you believe you're the *only* man in my life. Don't think I'm your personal...well, shall we call it, fun...girl?"

He gave her a double take. Her words had been biting. She had meant to cut, deep. Right between his legs; hit his cocked-up ego.

She wiggled slightly, so that her body moved suggestively. That would sidetrack him. It was one thing to cut at him; another to ruin their relationship! Business was business!

"How about some more bugging-juice?" she asked, giving him one of her sexiest smiles, moistening her lips and looking sweetly at him.

He gazed back coldly. "Look baby, I'm not the dumb ass you think!"

Whatever that meant!

"Just cut out the crap, and act like a—lady! *If* you can!"

The waiter came by, and he ordered another round of Martinis. "Make the lady's extra-dry." Then he looked back at her. "What's gotten into you. You're mighty flippant today."

That was the trouble with men, you could push them so far. Even a jackass like Willy.

"Okay, I'm sorry," she grumbled.

She couldn't afford getting on the wrong side of him. That was for sure.

"Just call it nerves...overwork." She reached out and took hold of his hand. "Forgive me?" Then kicked off her right shoe, placed her toes between his legs.

"Has nothing to do with it. Of course...but, damn it all, Joan, I...well, drop it!" Her wriggling toes were obviously exciting him.

The drinks came.

Before she realized it the glass was empty. Pulling out the olive and placing it in the ash tray with the others; absently counted.

Four.

Four drinks already and she was hardly feeling a thing.

Two drinks would have flattened her into a dead-headed body, walking around zombie-like for hours, a year ago.

Now four hardly worked at all.

It was like getting hit so many times in the same place that finally there is a numb spot, and nothing affects it anymore.

And she needed something to hit her, hard. It was going to be one hell of a long day.

"How about tonight?" Willy asked, squeezing her fingers. He caressed them roughly, and then tried to smile. But he was thinking too seriously about the very serious—to him—prospect of seducing her; and her caressing toes were teasing pleas for attention.

That did it!

Her fingers withdrew.

Thank God she did have something on for the evening.

"Sorry, baby...some other time, maybe?" she decided. She could hardly wait for Barry.

He shrugged as if it didn't matter in the least. "Well, if things a change between now and then stop by my place, and we'll have a little hot party of our own..."

Yeah, she could just see it! His idea of a party was stripping first thing, right off, and making with the quickies, between cocktails. Yesterday it wouldn't have seemed such a bad idea.

An inner shudder ran through her. *What she had to do for business...Who are you kidding? You like it—even with Willy!*

And that's what made Joan hate herself so much. Hate Blacky Jenson, too, for his filthy business, his clawing little, pudgy fingers that had promised her great riches if she only satisfied their hunger. Thank God for Ann. That woman had really knocked Blacky's balls off!

That had been the end of Joan. Three months as his mistress and she was finished; thrown to the boys, and her own means of support.

She felt sorry for Ann Cummings, his new blonde "baby-doll."

"Oh, baby-doll," he called and cooed and honeyed about with every lovely little female creature he used. "Baby-dolly, you and me are going places...I can see it in your eyes...in my heart!" His heart was centered in his pecking pecker. His so-called private-parts became public toys for the girls to pleasure night and day.

That was Blacky. He got a kick, during the end of a relationship—when he was about to dump a girl—by insulting her in public, when his henchmen were around, by saying things like: "She's a hot, all screwing mad. She could knock all of you guys off in one night and not even be satisfied."

In private he'd get cruel during intercourse; slapping her face when near a climax; or clawing her breasts or fanny so hard that it went beyond the point of pleasure-pain.

50

The last few times with him, he had thrown her over his lap and slapped her again and again with his hard, big hand. A couple of times he'd grabbed her head and slapped it a couple of times, then pushed it between his naked legs, saying:

"Meal time!"

Blacky could truly be a real bastard. He used women like cars and got new models fast, dumping the old girl. He didn't have any heart at all!

Someone should kill him. Someone should de-ball him. Slice him up for his race track business, his dope smuggling, his call girl racket, his political dabbling, and most of all for the perverse thrill he got in turning nice, innocent girls into whores.

Maybe some day she would get sick enough of this life not to care anymore. If she did, then would be the end of Blacky Jenson. At least then she would be able to die feeling she'd lived for some reason—some good reason. He deserved to die. In the most painful way.

She hated him more than she hated this little slob of a man sitting eagerly across from her, thinking of the exciting things he might do with her, if she would throw it at him.

She hated all men for what they had made her into.

All but Barry Davis. He was different. He at least played the game of showing respect towards her as a woman and fellow human being.

Oh, but he was so different!

* * * * * * *

Angrily, Barry moved the throttle in deeper, and pulled the plane into a high climb.

The flying didn't really do any good.

Women like Joan, who threw their bodies at any man just for the kick of it, made him feel cheap. Though he had to admit that Joan was pretty damn nice. And yet in a way a pitiful woman.

His mind returned to the blonde haired girl. He was still dazed with the memory of that embrace. The wild excitement. And something else…

What?

There was another nagging emotion. A haunting need he didn't know if he liked or not. A craving that was something other than physical, sexual, or animal. It was an angry-tenderness.

That was a thought: *angry-tenderness.* But that's the way he felt. Angry about the wild, protective tenderness she had inspired.

The plane cut into a cloud, and then suddenly was out of it.

Clear sky continued to the edge of space. He wished he was piloting a rocket, instead of Nelly. Flying in orbit...

"No reflection on you, old girl," he affectionately murmured, patting the control board.

Maybe if he could zoom out into space, into the black infinity, the airless emptiness between the planets...maybe then there would be rest.

To look down upon the planet earth from that height could wash away real attachment to the human race. It would stop the personal anguish from being a strong power over him. He would be able to look back and laugh.

Laugh at the millions and millions of people with their own little struggling, petty problems that have been blown-up in their minds to such a gigantic size that they can't seem to cut their way out...People like Joan, lonely; crazed for a man's real love.

Laugh, he told himself, and realize how unimportant man's struggle is. Laugh; and see the smallness of his world. The little pebble it is in the eyes of the universe. A grain of sand.

Laugh and know that his own ache, his own frustrations weren't important.

Scream a bitter laugh, because you can't do that. Because you're bound to this little speck of dust. Cry deep inside, because to you your problems *are* important. Very important, and they can't be run away from; escaped.

Yes, laugh and don't do anything but struggle in your sticky mire of glue that holds you like a pin was stuck through your chest, and all the effort and all the reaching out, won't get you anywhere.

Laugh, buster, because that's the only real way around that ache.

Laugh because you can't really do anything else and remain sane.

Gently, he slid the nose of his plane on a level with the ground, which stretched out like a long, wide, open expanse under him. The ground had no personality now. It had no life. It was nothing but ground, endless in all direction.

Yet down there were thousands of men getting hard up at the sight of hot woman.

Everybody had their hang-up; their sexual need. The perverse and frantic hungers to be satisfied in sexual union in a desperate attempt to escape the real problems of the world.

And he'd screwed it silly with a lot of broads. From hard case, cheap whores to women like Joan.

His mind jarred back to his immediate surroundings; taking in the endless blue sky that stretched out in all directions.

Below him, the world had become a mass of mountain-shaped clouds, giving the impression he was flying over a far distant planet, covered with fleecy, alien snow-covered land.

The sight inspired him; build a quick sense of pleasure; tore all thoughts of the perverted world below. Down there were the insane wars, the impossible violence. Great leaders were cut down by insane men. And what was left were the sick, sugar-sweet-mouthed, ignorant talking political would-be presidents that spoke like a Hitler, in words of childishly damned hatred for his fellow man. These bastards lived to be able to spout-out their perverted-hate insanity to fools stupid enough to believe this was their man and they were his loving people. Such perversions of life made the world a sick place to live in. Such men made a Hitler seem like an innocent child; caused one to think of the days of the Roman Empire, and its orgiastic Games, as tame as a cocktail. This was a world where married couples swapped mates, cheated on each other, went to church to find some kind of forgiveness their sins, so they could go off and screw the world for the next six days of the week. For these people their Church was a place to buy "spiritual" insurance, so that no matter what they might do in everyday life it was possible to be for-

53

given when death ended their life. Next to those people Joan seem almost saintly; because regardless of all else, she was honest with herself. No bullshit. No perverse religious crap to excuse even more perverse acts against everybody around them. People always found reasons, excuses, for doing whatever they wanted to do to satisfy their basest desires. The world was a cesspool, peopled by crummy little germs feeding on one another.

Up here, in the skies, was a real spiritual experience. Here was where all these angers and torments slipped away from Barry like dirt under the pressure of a hot shower. Here he was cleaned of all those feeling of being no better than the rest of the perverted world below.

Here he was made saner.

Flying alone like this was *his* spiritual bath; but the kind that didn't ask for forgiveness or attempt to fool himself that what he did in life was right. It was his way of escaping the pressures of being a lonely island in a sea of humanity, just as dirty as those around him.

This kind of experience, for Barry, was the only way he knew to even come close to wholeness; filling his complete being with a detached sense of freedom.

Up here he was alone, but in a greater sense, a real part of the universe—even able to believe that there was a God that loved all people, regardless of their sins; or faults.

Maybe, in a way, it made him feel just a tiny part of the Creator, blessed by the mere glow of His closeness.

He raised the nose of his plane at a high angle, as if reaching for the moon, the planets, racing out of the galaxy and into the arms of something bigger than himself, cleaner, pure and innocent.

The feeling was slowly coming, swelling up inside him like a wonderful full re-birth.

It is coming, his mind cried happily.

His heart was pounding like a glad bell inside him. It was beginning to ring deep and loud like an explosion that sang out—and finally he was free—for the moment.

Free, at last, of all the bullshit, crap, horrors of everyday existence; of struggling to just survive. Here he was something special in the universe; one with it!

And he was suddenly cut loose from the bonds of earth. Abruptly sliced away from all humanity and embraced in the arms of pure, innocent love.

Alone with his God and the universe.

Alone with good old Nelly, the only girl who had ever been a really true friend.

Then he remembered the girl, the blonde innocence who had made him feel almost this same way.

But he still didn't even know her name. Not even her name!

Chapter *SEVEN*

It was dark. Already dark. And a bunch of sexy whores for cargo. A cargo of sex. Fly a few girls in for a three point landing. Get a thousand dollars, and maybe you might have enough money to afford one of them.

He was sick of the whole business. And that blasted blonde girl, whose name he still didn't know. All he knew was that she lived at the house near the hangar. Blacky Jenson's house. One of Blacky's houses.

Houses.

That was a rotten one. Poor little old Nelly, turning into a house for the call girls of B.J. business operations that said: *Barry Davis, you just take my girlies out to this place to-night, and hand them over to the man in charge...*Poor old Nelly!

He had hated to call Joan, cutting the date. He had hated it because she was a good outlet for his guts that cried for Blondie.

Blondie! That's the only name that he had for her. The girl of blonde innocence that is an easy make.

That one hurt.

"How much further?" said the hawk-faced Denny Benton from behind.

The hawk-face he had taken Joan away from the night before. The man hadn't said anything about it, yet. But he was definitely cold. A cold but very efficient house-man.

He had arrived at the air strip early. Barry had hardly landed his little old Nelly when Hawk-Face showed up with a load of hot ladies that just couldn't wait to get with it.

"How soon can we take off, flyboy?" the man had sneered the moment Barry had gotten within hearing distance.

"Right after I refuel, if you're in a hurry."

"Snap to!"

And that had been that.

His mind was brought back to the present by the man's insistent voice. "Hey, flyboy," Denny Benton repeated from the door which led to the passenger compartment. "I asked you a question. Out with it! How soon do we arrive?"

He had to restrain himself from turning and smashing the man's face in. "About an hour now shove that head of yours out of here before it gets redesigned!"

There was a long, dead silence. "I hear you right, *Mister Davis.*" The words were slow and choppy.

"Blast off, pimp!" Barry cried over his shoulder, not even giving the man the honor of looking his way.

"You bastard! You...dirty no good, flying son of a bastard!" A heavy hand smashed across Barry's head.

He reacted faster than he'd ever moved in his life. One hand flipped across the control panel, expertly and speedily switching the plane to automatic, while at the same time he bodily stood, twisted and swung with his right arm.

The blow connected under the surprised and unexpecting jaw of the other man. He moaned as his teeth crushed together. Barry's other fist was already sailing in the direction of the man's stomach. It contacted and dug in deep and hard, carrying all the force in his body. Every nerve was in those two explosive swings; every built up anger, torment and fury.

Benton folded up, falling backwards into the passenger compartment with a sobbing groan. The expression on his face showed shock and astonishment and pain. The muscles of his mouth twisted in agony and his eyes were squinting with a moist smarting. Then he gasped for a long moment, trying to catch his breath.

There was a stunned silence in the air. Nobody was speaking; or hardly breathing. Only the sound of Benton trying to regain the air in his lungs.

Blood was trickling down the man's lips.

Finally, very slowly, with great effort, Hawk-Face started breathing in long, racking coughs. "Damn...damn..." he sputtered after several moments, as Barry looked on.

"You didn't...have to do that none!"

"You so much as try anything like that again and I'll kill you. Got me?" Barry snapped.

"Sure. Sure thing. Guess things just got out of hand a bit. There was a slight sound of an undercurrent of respect; as if the man was seeing him in a new light of understanding. "Sure thing. Sorry, didn't mean anything by it none. Nothing at all!"

So much for mister Hawk! Barry thought as he took the pilot's seat again. So much for his crap!

* * * * * * *

The voice had been doom in her ears. It cut through her like a stabbing knife. And that was ridiculous. Sure, she had counted on it. She had planned...Her day had been a hell and a delight all at the same time because Barry was going to be with her that evening. The knowledge had brought an anxious throb inside which had been enough to keep her alive for the first time in her life.

"I'm sorry, Joan," Barry's voice had said over the receiver. "But Blacky has a job..." and he didn't really sound so sorry. Not too regretful. It sounded faraway. Distant. And for some reason that hurt.

"Oh, it doesn't matter. Really!" she lied, trying desperately not to sound as if it bothered her in the least. She couldn't let him know how much it did upset her.

"Look, I'll call you up, later...okay?"

"Sure, sure—you do that!"

That was it. Crushed. Away. Finished. Gone. That was life!

She knew that she had been looking forward to Barry coming back that night, but had not realized how much.

She was still a sucker for a man—the right man. What was getting into her? One night, and *bang!* She was hit with a hammer, numbing her reasoning.

Shaking herself, she walked to the bar and mixed a drink. A large one. Strong. Straight. Something that would flatten her out on her back and make her not care anymore. A drink like she usually always had. One which cut away shame. Drowned the pleading inside her which cried so wildly for a man. Any man.

Escape. Escape from what she didn't like. Escape from what she couldn't face. "That's the way it goes, Dearie!" she cursed out loud, starting to gulp the contents of the glass.

She didn't even bother with ice any more. She didn't even bother to excuse it as a nightcap, an eye-opener, a booster or a drink before dinner. No reasons except that she wasn't caring and didn't want to care and didn't care about even thinking about it anymore.

The liquor hit her. Her stomach. Her nerves. Her muscles. The buzz began to move through her every cell. Her head, her brain, her desires. She was heated already.

What to do?

It had been a bad day. Hard. Tiring. Hot. Long. And Wilmore. Willy.

Will-the-pill! That was a laugh. And she didn't know why. It wasn't funny. It was the truth. Maybe that was why it was so funny.

Her hand ran along the curve of her hip. She had a good figure. One men wanted. And a strong sex-drive.

She felt herself going tense. It was starting.

That grind. That ache. The sickness that was like a burning plague heating her body.

And when her body hurt like that there was only one way to release and soothe the hurt. And the way she felt right then anybody would please her.

Her fingers clutched the glass in her hand, tight.

She squeezed harder on the glass; then too hard. Suddenly it and the contents were splattered on the far wall. The Scotch dripped slowly down toward the floor.

"Screw the fucking world!" She screamed. *That didn't do much good!*

Angrily she picked up another glass and filled it. Downed several gulps and waited. Waited for the soothing heat to work faster and faster through her blood.

There it was again. The way she needed a copout. The way she didn't want it, but was helpless to control.

Gulping a few more large swallows, she put the glass down and walked over to the phone. What difference did it make? Why should she care what it was, how it was; or who? One man should be as good as another.

She needed a real man. Like last night. Like all the nights before.

She picked up the phone. Dialed: Willy-the-pilly... Willy-nilly!

She couldn't help the laughter shaking her. Not humor, but bitter, bitter anguish. Because she had finally reached the point where even that slob was desirable to her. Because she would take up with anyone that wore pants.

Damn Barry! And you too, bastard Blacky Jenson!

* * * * * * *

It was bad weather. Real bad. But then, that was typical of San Francisco. Barry hadn't been to the place since the war, and only then when his ship happened to stop for a short weekend. Yet, even the fog had been over the city like an ugly curtain. Hiding.

He poured the contents of his drink down his throat. It hit, but had no real effect. Just so much water.

The last twenty minutes it had been a rough flight. Almost blind. And he didn't like flying blind. Then there was that Hawk-Face—Denny Benton. Things had cleared slightly with that man; just a change of attitude the guy showed.

"Hey," he called over to the bartender. "Another." He tapped the edge of the empty glass.

"Okay, buddy, just keep your shirt on!" the man snapped, moving slowly along the bar toward him.

He was taking his damn time! One punch in the face, and you'd be flattened out, bar-man!

What the blazes was bugging him? He felt like everybody was out to put the sword into his back. He'd been this way ever since he'd met that crazy blonde who kept running away. She was like a haunting nightmare. He couldn't get her out of his mind.

That was the trouble with having nothing to do with yourself. You started thinking. Tick. Tick. Tick went the brain, repeating the same old thing, the same old song...

I've heard that same old song before—too many times!

Boy meets girl. Boy falls in love. Girl runs away.

"Here y'are, buddy," the bar-man announced, shoving a new Scotch at him. The man pushed it along the counter as if afraid of getting too close to him.

Everybody seemed to know he was something dirty. The dirt must show on his face. His expression. Dirty business man. Sex jockey.

Eagerly he gulped the drink. *Nothing!*

Trouble with him, he needed a girl to burn out the disgust, and anguish, the...what?

Blondie, oh, Blondie where are you? In brother Black's little home, living it up

Blondie!

His hand crushed inward on the glass and smashed it to the bar. Some of the Scotch slopped over the edge and washed his fingers.

"Say, I was wondering if I'd find you here," a voice interrupted his thoughts. It was thick and over-friendly. "Look, let's bury the knife and act like we were old pals...I made a mistake about you—you seem an all right guy!"

He turned.

Hawk-Face!

"Well, hi there, old Hawky!" he grinned, taking the man's hand warmly in his, and patting him on the back. "Come on, let's have a blast-out together. Really oil the old burners together!"

The man foolishly smiled back. His eyes were already beginning to glaze. He wasn't aware of the sarcasm in Barry's voice. "Sure thing. After all, we work for the same man. Just got off to a bad start." He rubbed his chin thoughtfully, then grinned. "That was some punch you gave me!" Then he slammed into the bar stool next to Barry. "Friends?"

"Why...man, like crazy!"

Like I hate your guts, but anyone is better than no one...and you're almost no one—just not quite!

"Like buddy, old pal, what's to do around this town?" Barry asked.

Might as well make the most of it. A sap like this was the type to love your guts, after you've beaten his out of him.

The man turned and looked at Barry in a funny way.

One giant question mark for an expression, that said he must be a fool. "You kiddin'?"

"Me kid?" Barry cried in mock friendliness. "Me, kid *you*? Heck, I couldn't do that!"

"This town is wide-open. Flyin' with hot girls just hungry to screw." He tapped the counter with a fifty cent piece to get the bar-man's attention.

"How's that? Then what are we doing here bringing out-of-town girls?" Barry asked, now honestly interested.

"Big business. For one thing, they are protecting their men...a strange out-of-town whore is out of reach—nothing complicated can happen. They entertain clients with hot ladies, then split the scene with the girls. Anyway, out-of-town whores are better than the ones you can screw in your own back yard. It all has to do with keeping the girls away from the men afterwards. At least, that's what Blacky says. So that nobody knows or has a screwing chance of knowing who anybody else really is—a crazy business; but we cut into a lot of loot. And who cares? Big bucks make our wallets fat! Whatever their reasons are...we profit. A lot of loot!"

"Sure...a lot of loot!" Barry was still a little on edge.

Maybe a drink. Another drink; and then another and then another.

He was in a bad way. He'd always been able to handle his liquor, but tonight was worse. He was over-handling it, and the way he felt, it would take one hell of a lot to get him where he wanted to go. Out! Completely out. Like a light.

"Bar-man, a drink for my buddy here, and a shot of 151 proof rum for me."

Barry felt a mental jolt. That was pure poison. "How do you manage *that?*" he inquired, looking carefully at the man for the first time. His face was pure red. A violent crimson.

"You mean the Rum?" Hawk-Face grinned proudly.

There was no doubt that he'd hit the man's favorite subject—probably the only one outside of women and money. The man's eyes showed extreme interest.

"That's the only way to fly. If you really want to kick the hell out of it, burn all the lights and roll yourself flat." He paused and looked at Barry's drink. "What are ya drinking? Scotch, isn't it?"

He nodded.

"That'll mix. Real great! Try it out for size!"

The bar-man arrived with their drinks.

"Fix a shot of 151 Rum for my friend, here."

"Hey! Wait..." Barry started to protest, then decided it didn't really matter. He wanted to buzz out. He didn't have to worry about the plane flight until noon the next day.

The shot of Rum came and Benton told him to dump it in with his Scotch. He was about to point out this was a good way to ruin the whisky, but changed his mind. Why not try something really new. He did the deed. Downed part of the drink. Tasted it.

"Like Jamaican Rum—if I'm not wrong. Tastes just like it!"

"Right!" Benton agreed, finishing his own drink in one gulp and ordering another. "Say, want some screwing fun tonight? Something to kill the evening?"

"Sure thing..."

The drinks were beginning to explode his nervous system into a larger size. A size that wouldn't be restrained without some excitement. "Like what?"

"Girls? Hot ones!"

That was a thought! "Where?"

"Oh, I got some contacts here in Frisco. We can get a couple of chicks for a few bucks. What do ya say?"

Barry gulped the last of his drink. It would help make his choice for him. *He had never had to drop that far down to get girls, but.... It was a crazy thought. Take a plane load of dolls from L.A. to Frisco, and end up having to buy some local trash...That was a laugh!*

So what! What a combination of liquor. A real buzz juice. A great happy-time. He almost felt good. Almost felt happy. Almost felt like he could stand this bastard for the rest of the evening. If there were any girls around.

"Where do we go?" he asked.

"Well, first out of this airport, and into town. Then...No. Better make the call from here. Never can tell what direction we might have to take...be back in a minute!" Benton got up from the bar stool and walked across the room toward the telephone booth.

While he waited, Barry ordered a shot each of Scotch and 151 Rum. "Mix it together over ice...and...while you're at it, add a little Jamaica Rum!" The man gave him a look as if he were crazy, but he didn't give a damn.

Why not live it up? he thought while awaiting the return of his "friend."

By the time Benton got back he was beginning to really feel higher than the space satellites. His brain cells were spinning orbital things that rammed against each other, sending beautiful, colored stars exploding crazily before his eyes.

That last drink had done it!

Chapter *EIGHT*

The apartment was a cheap affair. Old furnishings. Darkly lighted. It was one of those places in the lower end of Mission Street, and you couldn't get much worse.

But then, what had he expected?

The girls were cheap. Worn out. Tired. Bored. All pro-whore. They didn't wait to build up anything. They were ready when the two of them arrived.

Benton had made one quick phone call and off they had started. Rented a cab and twenty minutes or so later here they were.

Two low-class prostitutes. Bleached blondes. Their bodies were old before their time, having reacted to the kind of life they lived.

Hell, what difference did it make? His mind hadn't been working since he'd left the bar. He couldn't care less.

And that was a lie.

He pushed that thought down into a dead-end slot of his brain.

Good! That's where it belonged. Lost. *Forgotten!*

You sure picked some dillies, Hawky, old boy.

"Hi boys," one of them had said when they arrived. He couldn't remember if it was the one rubbing her pitiful body against his or not.

It didn't matter.

Nothing was important.

He suddenly felt the bite of the woman's teeth. It was a harsh, painful grind. But he returned the kiss, running his hands hotly along her form.

All-in-all, he would not look upon her likes again—he prayed to his Maker he never would have to.

She was quite a step below Joan. Joan. It would have

been different with her. Not much. Just more interesting. She had better material. She cared more about it. And she was somewhat beautiful.

Not that *this* little bitch didn't care. She was oversexed enough and all that. But there was something disgusting about her.

The moment the door had closed on the apartment and they were safely inside, the girls had quickly pulled aside the robes they wore. After that, when Hawky eagerly grabbed for the one, it was just a matter of getting on with the deed. Well, it helped some. It took away the ache inside him. A frustrated ache that was now confused.

Joan. A body. A woman who knew *what* she was, and seemed to hate it. He had seen that in her eyes the morning after.

Just this morning? It was hard to believe so much had taken place in twelve hours. It was surprising how a man's life could change. His interest. His hungers. His passions.

Joan-the-Body, that relieved the sex tension. That was her.

And the blonde innocence? Blondie! What about her? Who was she with tonight? What new man was with that delicate perfection

It sickened him to think about it. He tried pushing the thoughts out of his mind, and tried to concentrate on what he was doing. What he was trying to escape with.

Escape. There was that word again. That was life. He escaped from himself and the dirty life he was living by taking the first girl that came along. He escaped from his emotions that became frightened of the blonde girl—afraid that he felt something more important than just sexual attraction. Escaped because he couldn't have her—couldn't even learn her name.

And now, he escaped from his escape—Joan.

He didn't have Joan. His outlet. So he took up with this little, pitiful thing, that knew nothing else but sex. That could do nothing else. And would die with nothing else accomplished.

Joan had her photography. She was a failure in what she had started out to be: *a glamorous movie star.* But she had

66

found another level of success. Two successes really. Her business; her body. A handy woman to have around; and her business was taking pictures.

Escape to Joan because you can't have the blonde girl.

Escape to a cheap professional because you can't have Joan.

And for heaven's sake, escape from yourself because *you* too have failed. You failed to become what you wanted to become.

And what was that?

A fireman. Policeman. President of the United States?

He had forgotten long ago. So long ago that all memory had left. Maybe it had been a doctor, or author, or actor.

Maybe a lover!

That last would have been fine! Ending by paying a worn out lady to give the love...that could be real *success!*

But he had grown up and suddenly found himself in his own created trap.

The insistent pressure of the woman's body pressed his thoughts back to her. She moved in a mechanical fashion, meant to arouse desire in him. Meant to create the fire of passion. A passion that he couldn't stop. It was purely automatic biological release.

Take her, and be done with it. Screw her fast and cruel.

Violently.

Take her like he'd screwed no other woman before. No thought of her, no interest if she liked it or not. Not caring any more. She was there to please him. And damned if she wouldn't do just that!

His way!

* * * * * * *

"Ann Cummings on the phone," Joan Verril heard her secretary say over the receiver.

"Put her through..." Her head was aching. The first time in months. She was almost glad. A good old hangover. What she needed to take her mind off other problems.

"Hello, Joan?" the mellow voice said in her ear. It jolted right through her system.

"Keep it down, honey, I'm hung-over."

"Oh, sorry," the voice said, softer. A laugh seemed hidden in it.

Joan offered: "Okay, so I've done gone out an' done it. Nothing new, honey. What you want?"

There was a pause. A long silence. She could hear the other woman's breath. "Could I...could I see you sometime today?"

Joan thought that over. She felt sorry for Ann, but she also felt something else. *Envy?* Maybe. She didn't know. The girl had an innocent brightness about her. Unspoiled. A quality which Joan had lost a long time ago. Two months? Three? A year?

It seemed several centuries ago.

She had made good in a business already overloaded. Within months. And only because she had a jump on most other photographers. She knew the business well. And that body of hers.

But Ann hadn't changed any since she had first met the girl about twelve months ago. They had both had a bit-part in a movie together. They came to the conclusion that they didn't have any talent in acting at about the same time. Then she hadn't seen Ann for a while, during which it was big, beefy Blacky Jenson and his promises. Then Joan had seen her and they'd started getting together once in awhile, and finally Ann met Blacky.

That was the end of Joan.

Ann had taken over. But by then it didn't matter any more. She had been glad to get out. The blonde was welcome to him.

But she felt sorry for the girl. Now *she* was in the man's clutches; and still holding desperately to that clean honest side of herself. It would be killed after awhile. It couldn't stay alive with her surroundings.

Yes, she felt damn sorry for the kid. "Sure, hon...around three. Okay?"

"Thanks," the voice almost cried with relief.

* * * * * * *

The flight back to Los Angeles was a slow, painful experience. Barry was mentally cursing Hawk-Face all the way for that terrible combination of *Scotch and 151 Rum.* But he had been too high when Benton suggested it to refuse. Then —*bang!*

He remembered something about spending most of his waking hours in the arms of some girl. Or was it two? Arms. Breasts. Lips. Hips. Legs.

That's all he remembered. But it was enough! Somehow the two of them had made it back to the plane. Why the plane neither had been able to remember. They had awakened in the morning around ten.

And what a head he had grown during the night. Two heads. Whoever said that two heads were better than one had never experienced a true, splitting hangover!

But finally the trip came to an end. The sky had been clear all the way down the coast. That was a blessing.

He jumped behind the wheel of his car. Started and directed it toward the highway. He had planned stopping at the house near the airstrip to look up Blondie, but decided that he wasn't in any condition to be looking up anybody. He needed a shave. A bath. Clean clothing. And about twenty-four hours of sleep. Maybe then he'd feel more like living it up. Looking around for Blondie.

He was one hell of a copper-brain. Without even knowing her name he was thinking about her all the time.

A stab of physical and mental pain moved through him. He'd just received a distorted mental picture of the woman he'd been with the night before and it made him sick. Whatever it was he had been pawing seemed hardly human in his mind now—not that he'd been particularly impressed with her bodily form last night either. But a nipple was a nipple. And the rest of her body parts functioned.

Thank you, mister...it's over!

He liked sex. But not in the raw like last night.

Joan. Yes. That was different. Joan had something else besides her drinking and sex. If nothing else, a good body. A cheap pickup. But with guts. *That was it!*

He wondered what the blonde would be like.

And he knew. She would be different, too. But different

from *all* the rest. Completely different.

Tender. Kind. Delicate. Emotional. Exciting.

Wonderful. Lovely. *Love!*

Don't tell *me*, Mister Davis—Barry Davis, man around town, sworn bachelor, never to get seriously interested—is suddenly seriously interested!

That did it! No more thinking?

Still he couldn't get the image of that beautiful face from in front of his eyes. It was dear. Kind. Understanding. Sensitive. Wide innocent eyes. Love of life. *He was an all day sucker for a beautiful face. A beautiful woman. A beautiful body.* And this girl had all of that, and lot more.

Intelligence.

Cut it!

That blasted head. It would need a couple of aspirin to deaden the agony. He was thinking too hard. His brain hurt. The temples throbbed. They burned. They beat like a pulsing fire had been built behind them. They pushed outwards, as if trying to explode.

He'd have to do something about that. And fast!

* * * * * * *

Ann had on a bright summer dress. One thing Joan could say about this girl was that she knew how to dress to fit her personality.

"I hope I'm not being too much of a bother," she smiled across the table. They were in one of the many catch-a-quick-lunch and coffee-break places with atmosphere and cocktails, which Hollywood featured.

"Don't be silly," Joan exclaimed, brightly. She was glad that Ann had called up. It had been quite a long time since the two of them had had lunch or any meal or length of time to visit together.

She decided she really liked the girl. You could not help liking her.

But then, on the other hand, she liked everybody today. Ever since Barry had called. That had been just before Ann had showed up at her studio.

"Hi, baby!" His voice had said cheerfully. "What's

70

new?"

"Nothing much!" At first she'd been a little cool, while her heart was beating faster and her blood started flowing wilder.

He had that effect on her.

"Just got back to my room. Pretty messy day yesterday. Sorry about last night. But that's the way things go."

"Sure..." she let her voice trail off. She'd be damned if she'd make it easy for him.

"How about tomorrow night? Have anything on?"

She thought it over. It made her a little irked to think he had the idea she was such a pushover. Yet, how could she blame him. She'd all but thrown herself at him that first night. Under Blacky's orders...but he didn't know that!

"Nothing on..." she sighed.

"Well, how about nine?"

That was subtle. Nine. Too late for dinner. But early enough for cocktails and a few free-feels. Just like all the others.

Not quite! "Okay, nine."

"Swell."

And that had been that. Except it had changed her whole day. The hangover left. The depression. The anger.

So now she loved everyone. Even Ann who had taken...Hell, she should be crazy about the girl for having gotten her out from under Blacky's fingers.

"I didn't know," she was saying to Joan, "if I should come to you about this. It's just that—well, we have known each other for some time, and you were in the same situation I'm now in and well, maybe you could give me some advice."

Sure, the advice girl, Joanie Verril, who has made such a wonderful thing out of her own life.

Miss Successful Playgirl of Twentieth Century.

"What is it?"

"Two things, really..." Ann was looking down at her half empty plate. Nervously. Her fingers working with the fork. She looked up and then around the small restaurant. Nobody was looking their way. She seemed to be relieved. "About this pilot."

That jarred Joan. She hadn't expected Ann even to know about him. Except through the business...maybe that was it. Blacky was sending her out to do the dirty questioning. Find out if he's a real man. Find out if he can be trusted. Discover what he thinks, what he says.

What, what, what!

She felt an icy chill run through her. This was one hell of a dirty trick to pull on a nice little girl like Ann. A rotten trick. "What about him?" Joan asked evenly, as if she had no idea of what to expect.

"I understand...well, you...you had him up to your apartment."

"Yes..." here it came.

"Could you...I mean..." She was silent for a moment. A long, awkward moment. "We've been friends a long time. You know how it is," she began again, more sure of herself, more controlled. She was started and wouldn't stop now. "You know how it is with Blacky. You get trapped and can't get out. You get into the bind and want out, but are afraid of making the move. I tried once and found myself in the hospital for a couple of days. A girl just doesn't walk out on him..."

Joan nodded. She had heard about the beating Ann had gotten. At the time it sickened her. It sickened her now.

"Well, I've got to get out—one way or the other. There's no telling what he might do—I know he's been involved indirectly in murder and I'm honestly afraid of what he might...if I don't..." her voice was choked. Tears were moistening her eyes. "This is...silly I know but—damn!" She stopped long enough to pull out a Kleenex from her purse and wipe her eyes. "I...have to get out—or I'll be killed. I mean, what's left of what I brought of myself into Hollywood. This town eats you away. Then you meet a rat like Blacky and..."

Joan knew. And her insides hurt. Hurt terribly. One day, someone would kill Jenson.

Someone should. He had destroyed her. She knew what the boys thought and said of Joan Verril..."Keep her around for a good, fast lay!" That's all she was good for. And that's all Ann would be good for pretty soon. Jenson would tire of her, and then throw her to the trash which hung around him. Right now she was protected from them only because she was his woman. His mistress.

And only because of that.

"What I'm trying to say is arrange a meeting with Barry and me?"

She didn't have to ask why. She knew. Hire the man to fly her out of the city. Maybe out of the country. Far enough away so that Blacky couldn't get to her.

She didn't notice Ann's reference to Barry by name. She was too wrapped up. Later she would remember; but, now she was mad. Mad enough to do almost anything.

"Sure, sure." She thought it over. Not tonight; tomorrow maybe.

No! Talk to Barry about it, but keep him for herself. "I'll call you tomorrow—or the next day. Will that be soon enough?"

Ann nodded.

Chapter *NINE*

Drinks. Dinner. Drinks.

Nine o'clock. Dear old Joan. Time for screwing. Time for running around chasing yourself. Time for escaping. Momentarily black out.

But not final, complete escape.

After darkness comes light. From night to morning. And you get up and look at yourself in the mirror. And you think: *"There you are, you bastard. Just like before. Just like yesterday. You haven't gotten away. You can't!"* So you run like a rat in a maze, banging your head against blind alleys, but never finding a way out.

Joan was beautiful. That was one thing about her. Pretty and knew how to show off her sex. The blue dress she wore open in the front, just barely hiding her large breasts, but showing the long dip between them.

"Hi," she smiled warmly, stepping close. Her hips surged sensuously against his, soft, but intimate, like a woman who knows her man and wants to make it obvious how much she enjoys being a woman in every way.

Her hips moved, ever so slightly, but it was highly erotic, almost as if they were rubbing nakedly together.

She slipped her arms about his neck, her lips pursed against his.

"I've waited for you, Barry," she murmured against his cheek, her breasts soft and yielding as they cushioned against his.

The feel of her was erotic, but beautiful in a sexually exciting way. It was like holding someone you really cared about; who cared about you—but without any strings.

He slipped his right hand against the fullness of her breast, then under the top of her gown to discover she was

74

not wearing a bra under the dress. Her nipple responded to his intimate caress and her lips murmured in pleasure. He felt himself immediately getting hard in response. Her hips slipped from side to side against him.

"I *do* excite you, don't I?" she sighed, almost amused, but also very pleased.

"Can't you *feel* it?" He laughed, as they parted from the welcoming embrace.

"Sorta," she smiled, then patted his hip with the flat of her hand; it was an affectionate touch. "It's nice knowing how excited you get. But. First, how about some drinks. You look like you could use one!"

He merely nodded, patting her playfully on the fanny as she turned. Her responsive giggle of pleasure was very attractive.

After his Frisco night, Joan was a great change, a delight to hold and touch; surprisingly wonderful to kiss. And had some class about her.

He followed her across the room, watching the delightful sway of her hips as she swung them back and forth in a very natural, animal-like manner. It was a cat-like swing; rhythmic and graceful.

He realized that Joan had real class; not like the hard case whores he'd screwed in Frisco.

In the kitchen Joan asked: "Martinis?"

"Sure thing." Barry stepped up beside her as she started pouring the cocktail. He leaned close and tenderly ran his lips along the back of her neck, kissing the lobe of her ear, then caressingly tonguing her naked shoulder.

She murmured like a contented kitten.

But when he slipped his hand around, under her arm, into the depths of her plush neckline, exploring her fleshy breast, gently teasing the hardened nipple, Joan laughed in delight. It caused her breast to move excitingly against his hand.

"Hold on, lover boy..." she murmured, stepping gracefully away. "That's a terribly naughty thing to do to a girl when she's busy mixing cocktails!"

He laughed throatily. "And more than the liquid kind!"

Joan licked her lips, winking at him. "That is one cocktail I want to really mix, right. It's got to have the right power in it...liquid, fiery power! So it can really twist-up a storm!"

Laughing, delighted by the double-lined conversation, Barry threw back lightly: "And you are just about the greatest cocktail snatcher in the world!"

With a mock frown, Joan retorted: "Only 'about' the greatest snatcher?"

"Well," he shrugged, helplessly, "it takes all kinds, and...who knows who is the best?"

"Then, I'll just have to do my best to do a little convincing. After all, I'm the all-time play around girl. I have to keep up my scratching reputation!"

Barry couldn't help reaching out and squeezing her molded fanny where it pressed against the tight fitting dress.

"That's not nice!" she complained with a grin of delight.

Just for the hell of it, Barry placed his other hand against the front of her dress, letting his fingers slide slowly downwards..

"Hell, stop that!" she cried, almost spilling the cocktail she was in the process of picking up.

"Okay, if that's the way you feel about it!" Barry let his hand slide down in a quick caress, then fall to his side. He walked over to the large white sofa in the center of the room. "Next time *you* have to come to me."

Joan followed him, holding a cocktail glass in each hand, saying: "If you don't make me *come* I'd be a very surprised woman!"

She sat down next to him, handed over one of the martinis.

He said: "Joan, you look beautiful enough to eat!"

Her eyes flashed as she took a sip of the drink. Then she told him in a voice that was lustfully husky: "I certainly won't stand in your way. You can devour me. But," she added, looking down between his legs, "you better be prepared to be giving me a whale of a meal, too. I'm just starved!"

"We *could* go out to dinner," Barry suggested in a boyishly innocent voice.

"We're going *in* for a hot sexy dinner, honey, right

here!" was her quick retort. "At least *somebody* is going *in,* and I don't think I have the right equipment to be the *in* person...but I have a certain longing to invite a certain person I know to go *all the way* in! Full visiting rights—with complete authorization to search every piece of furniture, drawer, closet and room within my person! Total exploration and search rights!"

"You make that sound very inviting!"

"I thought you already found me very inviting. At least, I've never pulled the welcome mat away."

"I'd have nothing against you pulling it away—or is it the door that has to be *opened?*"

He tapped the edge of her dress, meaningfully. "You better the hell have something against it, when the door *is* flung open!" She giggled, happily. "You are crazy fun to be with."

"You're not so bad yourself!" Barry let his eyes run lingeringly along her voluptuous curvy body. "Come to think of it, you are just about the most delicious thing in the apartment. Just looking makes me *very* hungry! What you have is the tastiest food a person could desire to feast on."

"I'd debate that," Joan announced, placing her hand between his legs, then withdrawing it with a lingering caress. "That looks mighty delicious to me. A real feast!"

They both laughed happily.

In the silence that followed, Barry realized how much of a ball Joan was.

For some reason he felt he had known Joan for a long time now. They were old friends; buddies. Yet they had only known each other for a few passionate hours. It was strange how people shaped up. Here they were, almost strangers, yet there was that feeling between them. It was carnal, a friendly orgasm. But with an understanding of each other; acceptance of one another as human beings; emotional creatures.

With Joan it was this awareness. This bodily need for each other. If only for this moment, of course. In fact, that was it. Just *for* the moment. No strings attached.

Adults could be like that. Kids couldn't afford it. And how many children were there, in fully matured and aged bodies? A big breast on a woman's chest didn't mean that she was adult. That was something she couldn't help—she grew, she developed, she filled out, became overweight, started to show signs of old age and finally died. You can't help the changes in your body.

But you can help *not* growing up. Mentally. Emotionally.

With Joan.

It was sex. No bones about it. Nothing more. Maybe it was because of that quality that he felt so relaxed with her. Maybe that was why he liked her the way he did. She was a lot like himself in that way.

He knew what he wanted. He knew what he was. He tried to face it. And at times tried to run away from it. Yet, he didn't lie about himself to himself.

"You're mighty silent!" Joan's voice interrupted his thoughts. She was sitting on the couch next to him. Very close. He could feel her presence. He could smell it.

She handed him a glass. "I didn't bother with cocktail glasses...takes too long that way...and too much work refilling," she explained, as he looked at the large container that she had given him, filled with martinis.

"That's enough to rock off our heels!"

He felt her hand reach down between his legs, linger idly there. Her touch was sensual, but also nice, almost a kind of wholesome, an intimate love-act between two people who completely understood one another.

He sipped his drink, enjoying how her hand just lay his clothing.

Suddenly he felt restful, almost too relaxed and contented and realized he'd have to take it easy with the booze if he expected to enjoy the pleasure of Joan's body. He was already beginning to feel the effects of the liquor buzzing through his head.

As she slowly withdrew her hand, Barry's attention returned to the immediate present and he put his hand on hers. Joan's fingers were warm and gripped back with an intense longing.

She said: "It's so wonderful, Barry, having you here, like this."

"I'm glad...and happy you didn't have anything planned

for tonight," he whispered in a much too husky voice, looking into her eyes. "I was afraid you might be...involved with something else."

She shook her head, said: "Even if I had been I'd have broken it off, for you."

He leaned close, tenderly kissing her cheek. His lips ran along its velvet texture, down to the white cream of her smooth neck, then up towards her full mouth.

She surged eagerly closer, turning, in order to slide arms about his neck.

Then their lips met, open. He thrust his tongue into her mouth and she pulled it deeper, her lips sucking as if attempting to drain his flesh dry. It was a violent, but loving kiss and as he withdrew his tongue, hers followed his until it was filling his mouth. She trembled, tensely caressing the back of his head.

He felt as if all his nerves were bursting under the impact of the kiss.

Then, after a long voluptuous moment, they parted.

"Golly..." she murmured, breathlessly. "I can't take any...more of *that!"*

"How do you think *I* feel?" Barry managed to say in a very shaken voice. "Christ you kiss wild! "

A quick smile of pleasure crossed her lips. Without another word they slid down, full-length on the couch, her arms pulling him gently against her.

"Oh, I *love* having your body on me...like this," Joan whispered. Then she put her lips against his ear, very lightly sucking in. It sent a wave of thrilling pleasure through his whole body.

He was painfully aware of the softness of her flesh under him, hips longingly surging up.

"Oh, Barry, you feel wonderful."

Their lips fused, first gently, lovingly, then they were tongue kissing, but this time in thrusting moves that moistly pressed their tongues against one another again and again. Then suddenly she pulled his deeply into her, pressed it up hard under the roof of her mouth, lips violently sucking, her whole body rigidly squirming, her thigh thrust between his legs, wiggling, her breasts soft cushions of heaving flesh.

He almost felt an orgiastic come, then she relaxed slightly, released her hold on his tongue.

As their lips moved away from each other, his sliding down to her ear-lobe, she murmured, "Oh, Barry, you don't know what *that* did to me! It was like...having you in me! Downstairs!*"*

He worried Joan's ear-lobe with his lips and tongue, placed a hand against her breast, fondling. She surged up to meet the caress, a thigh thrust eagerly against him, moving back and forth.

"Oh, dear Barry, it's so good with you. You're so beautiful. For God's sake, I can't stand it any longer. Do something, quick, please!" she moaned, squeezing his shoulders with tormented fingers. "This is...*too* much!*"*

He lifted and her hands desperately undid his slacks, tore at the confining shorts. The touch of her fingers as they played against him created a quick response.

"My skirt..." Joan moaned.

The two of them awkwardly shifted so he could lift her skirt, then she raised her legs straight up in the air as he peeled off her tiny black lace panties, pulling them up over her full, voluptuous thighs, then along her tapered calves, all the time letting his hands make it a caressing, sensual action. When he'd pulled one foot free, Joan sobbed and merely dropped her legs on either side of him, thighs parted wide as possible. Hands urged him down to her; one now in full, thrilling possession of him, the other gripped excitedly on the back of his neck.

Their hips surged together and the first contact, flesh against flesh.

She moaned in contented pleasure.

"Oh, Barry, that feels so good...do it some more...that way." Her hands embraced the back of his neck, fingers tenderly caressing.

"So good..." she moaned as their hips took on a slow rhythm that moved them back and forth against one another.

Suddenly, like a possessed wanton, Joan choked out between clinched teeth: "Don't wait!*"*

As only two experienced lovers can, their hips made a quick sliding adjustment and he was suddenly half buried within the fire of her.

"Barry, Barry," she sobbed, choked with emotion and pleasure, *"Oh,* you are *so* good...so *good*...oh, *Barry!"*

Her hips thrust up, taking in the full length of him, twisting, circling.

He knew that Joan must have climaxed and also knew he wanted to make it very good for her. So he continued to play out the erotically stimulating circular movements her.

She was gasping, her face bathed in a lovely contented smile, eyes closed. And from this expression he knew how much pleasure she was experiencing.

For a long time he continued to tease and control the lovemaking; only now and then dipping deeper within her in tensely circular movements. Then he would pull out almost all the way, so that she could experience the most voluptuous pleasures.

Once again Joan gasped, deep-throated, her mouth wide-open in ecstatic joy, h suddenly grinding under him, jerking up and down, tugging and pulling, then slamming up to seemingly gulp-up all of him within her body.

Somehow, even amazing to himself, he managed to keep control as she convulsively experienced her second voluptuous climax about him. Then slowly he withdrew, plunged in again, lingeringly.

"Barry, you're...*kidding!"* she exclaimed from deep within her lungs. "Oh, *Barry*...what are you doing!"

He leaned over, kissed her lips, gently, but she opened her mouth and the invitation was too strong. She pulled his tongue deep, but tenderly, her own tongue stroking the bottom of his, pressing it against the roof of her mouth. Then she suddenly was voluptuously clutching with her lips, sucking violently.

The fire of that kiss drove him beyond the limits of control and his hips started hammering harder and faster, thrillingly thrusting himself again and again into her, until finally, after only moments, he felt the bursting release built. Every muscle tightened hard against the pleasure as it erupted throughout every nerve.

Her own motions, writhing, convulsively, revealed the voluptuous pleasure she experienced along with him.

Then they relaxed against one another.

It had been pure, animal heat, fantastically wonderful, but in a raw orgiastic way.

Yet gently loving until that final climax.

Finally they shifted to be able to lay side by side, cramped in the narrow confines of the sofa, but held so close together that their bodies seemed like one.

It had been wonderful, Barry realized. But in an erotic orgiastic madness, nothing more. No deeper emotions.

Moments of half-consciousness drifted by, then awareness of time and place returned.

As his fingers interlaced with hers, he couldn't help wondering how it would be with the blonde girl.

That was funny. She always popped up in his mind at the strangest times. Even now, right after making love to another woman. To Joan, the beautiful, orgiastic tramp in heat.

An eagerness seemed to be working through the woman clutched to him.

Joan, and her sex-filled body—poor Joan, who didn't even realize he hadn't been thinking about her.

He felt, more than saw, her reach out for him, mentally calling for his intimate body-embrace, physically demanding it. More tenderly this time, more softly, more temperately; but deeply passionate as before.

But this time Barry broke the embrace to glance in the direction of Joan's bedroom.

The moment they were on the bed, fully naked this time, the wildness of their rebuilt need burned quickly; as if the first session had been only a warm-up.

Her hands were all over him, caressing, fondling his body as much as his own hands were active on hers.

This time he smothered her breasts and nipples with voluptuous tongue-kisses. Her fingers found the length of his shaft, squeezing, rubbing, and lowering to discover the form and shape of his testicles. No verbal conversation was exchanged this time, not at the beginning, at least. There was a frantic desperation about their love-making, as if the only conversation had to be physical touches. When one was visibly thrilled by a caress or kiss or movement, the other's reaction shouted with more erotic efforts; but they were silent shouts.

Then, he was cross-wise to Joan, her fingers continuing to make love to him, while his kisses lowered from her breasts, slid along her stomach, then slowly lowered.

She sobbed at the erotic tongue-kiss. Her hands dragged at his hips until she had pulled him over her. His hands straddled her hips as she positioned his legs and thighs so that her face could raise up between them, hands clutching at the cheeks of his buttocks.

A moan sounded from Joan as her lips just breathed in around him. Then she was mouthing him, slowly tonguing what her lips so lustfully possessed.

They both went crazy with heat, lips pulsing orgastically upon the other's most erotic, intimate sexual possession.

And in the madness of it all there was also a fantastic beauty to their actions. He bathed in the joy of her, as continual waves of fiery pleasure surged through every nerve of his body. Then he felt them both climbing to the final ecstasy of white heat; *far* too soon!

* * * * * * *

It wasn't until late, very late, that Joan remembered about the request Ann had made the afternoon before. A request that had been urgent and desperate.

She didn't remember until their bodies were satisfied, and tired. Their minds happily relaxed. Their passions finished and spent out for the moment. Not until they were just silently enjoying the company of one another.

She could feel his hand twine to hers. It felt nice. Friendly warmth. She felt good now. Happy. Contented.

She looked at Barry, and liked what she saw.

He had a directness about him that showed in his face and eyes and actions. An honesty.

His hand clasped her fingers tighter. A thrill went up through her body like a slow, gentle wave. A thrill that was excitement but not sexual stimulation. She liked being touched by Barry. She liked being made love to by him. She liked him: period!

"Want another drink?" She leaned forward and picked

up the cocktail mixer. He nodded, and she poured some of the liquid into his glass.

"Stop!" his voice shouted in alarm, bringing the flow to a halt.

They sat silently for a while longer.

Not much had really been said since Barry had arrived. First that demanding passion that had ripped through them in a wild wave had to be answered. Now there didn't seem to be much to say. It had all been said with their passions, their bodies. As if that were the only level on which they could communicate.

It was moments like this that made life almost worth the effort it took to face each day. It helped to cut away some of the shame. She could easily be happy with a man like Barry.

Not Barry! He knew her for what she was. To him she was just another quick thrill. Maybe one that he enjoyed a little more than most. She hoped so. She liked to think so. She didn't know. But he deserved something better. He deserved someone like the girl she used to be. Clean and wanting to continue being so.

He would end up with someone like Ann Cummings. A girl who was adult, mature, and imperfect like Barry. But a girl that had the sensitive feelings he expressed and had; a girl that could still be class.

That's when she remembered.

"Say, Barry!" she exclaimed in much too loud a voice.

He moved sharply in surprise.

"Sorry. I just remembered something. There's this little girl who wants to see you. Ann...Ann Cummings. A blonde. Lives with Blacky. His mistress. They live out in the country place—where you keep your plane. You might have seen her. Very pretty. An angelic quality. Innocent-looking. Almost childlike."

He froze suddenly. Froze like ice. His fingers moved from hers. He seemed to shrivel inwards, as if shocked.

"Ann. Ann Cummings," he said softly, as if in a dream. Thoughtfully. "It fits her. Fits her, real nice." He seemed lost. Drifting into another world. One that was not hers to enter. A shell had enclosed him. A wall slammed down between the two of them. Cold.

84

A shudder ran through her.

He shook himself and looked eagerly at her. The eagerness wasn't for herself. It was for something else.

Someone else?

"What about her? She wants to see me? *Why? When? Where?"*

That was when she knew. And she didn't really know, at first, how the whole thing seemed to fit so nicely together—but it did—perfectly! Maybe she remembered something Ann had said at lunch. She had called him *Barry. By name!* Then this reaction of his. It fit. All of it. So revealingly.

And she felt ill. Very ill. It was too late to back out now. She'd have to answer his questions. She'd have to keep her promise.

She shrugged inwardly. After all, she had known it wasn't real. That it wouldn't last. That he was only interested in her body. To him, she was nothing but a hot cunt to fill with his prick! An emotional, sexual outlet.

But this thing with him and Ann. That really shocked her with surprise. That came as an unexpected, brutal jilt.

Too soon. *Too damn soon!*

Chapter *TEN*

The head. My kingdom for a head.

Barry woke. His brain felt like a blaring progressive jazz band was going full blast inside his skull. Over and over. Blast. Blast. Blast! A throbbing pain.

He was living in hangovers.

At first he couldn't remember where he was, or what had happened last. All that was left of him was the rhythmic pulsation of his own special brand of skull-hammers smashing from the inside, in their attempt to split his head outwards.

Then something about San Francisco. Then Los Angeles. Girls. Ann Cummings.

The name came like an explosion out of nowhere. It popped into existence out of black nothingness. The words didn't mean anything at first.

Just:

Ann.

Cummings.

A face started to fade in. A face surrounded with red hair that opened like a canyon. The mouth seemed to expand until it was gigantic. He watched with fascination as the monstrous tongue beckoned him in.

He shook his head.

That wasn't her!

He tried to collect his thoughts. Opened his eyes, and screamed inwardly. The lids squeezed violently shut. His head was splitting wide open, and carefully, in agony, he slid down into his bed, pulling the covers over him.

Hidden in the darkness again he could think, once the ache subsided.

Think. About. Ann Cummings.

Then the blonde-haired innocence did a quick fade-in job; weaved, blurred and then came into sharp focus.

Ann Cummings!

Blondie!

Ann Cummings!

He wanted to get up and dance, yell, sing, walk straight up the wall, across the ceiling and down the other side.

Hell and damnation...what was wrong with him? No girl had hit him like that. And that was what had shocked him the night before.

Her name is Ann Cummings, his mind had repeated over and over, as if he had been locked in a world of his own, just with that name and vision before him as a companion.

Bless Joan for telling him!

Then he had pulled out of it. He had moved away from that tight, confusing universe which had walled him in, away from humanity and reality. He had turned to Joan and flooded out the questions that had been tormenting him for the last few days. And then he had found out the ugly truth. The truth that had made him sick. And now added to his nausea, as he remembered.

She was Blacky Jenson's mistress. And that hurt. Terribly. To think of her in the gross little fingers of that bastard. It wouldn't take much to make Barry want to kill the man after hearing that. Stamp the life out of the guy with his bare fists.

Then there was a mixture of stories. Joan's story. Ann's story. They were intertwined. Mixed up because they seemed so similar. Yet, there was a difference. Ann wanted to get free. And it wasn't too late for her.

Sure, she'd made the mistake. Anybody could do that. He had known she was caught in a filthy trap. And in a way it wasn't quite as bad as he had first thought it would be. It was one thing to be like Joan, jumping in bed with every man, and any man, just for kicks. And quite another to be giving out to only *one*. One at a time, anyway!

But that *one!*

No wonder Ann had told him to get out while the getting was good. Maybe he would, after the next job. That would pay off Nelly, and he'd be in business for himself, with no overhead. Then he could tell Blacky and the whole group to shove it.

And good!

The phone rang. It was a spear through his head. It cut into his nerves like pure, raw aching fire. Moving through an island of agony he jumped from his bed and leaped toward the phone, which hung on the far wall.

"What the hell is that?" he yelled into the receiver. His skull was throbbing horribly again.

"Davis. That you?" came the voice. It sounded like Hawky. "This is Denny Benton. The boss wants to see you at noon—for lunch, and business."

"Okay. Okay..." he nodded, hanging up the phone without even saying another word or good-bye.

Then he froze.

He was supposed to have lunch with Joan and Ann today. That had been the arrangement last night. Now, smashed by Blacky. Jenson was getting in his way too much. First causing him to miss out on Joan that second evening— and now this.

The man was intolerable. The more relations he had with him, the more Barry disliked it.

Any person who would have a woman beaten up, just because she'd finished with him and wants to call it quits...*That bastard should be hung by his thumbs. Better yet, by his balls.*

The idea of being face to face with the man throughout a whole lunch made his insides grip. It would be hard to control himself. But, somehow, he would have to. Money was money. Later, maybe, he would have his day with Jenson.

Later—and that was a promise!

So it was a peaceful lunch with Black-the-Jack!

That's all he needed after last night, and his head, and the fact that he was missing out on his arranged meeting with Ann Cummings.

Stop it! Or you'll be in an uncontrollable rage

He hurt inside. His mind was an expanding, contracting thing on his shoulders. His mouth felt dry like sand paper; his nerves were shaved down to their throbbing cores.

He felt like hell.

All he needed was a gentle push!

Picking up the phone again, he dialed Joan's number. There was a long wait, then he heard her sleepy voice.

"Hi, baby...he muttered.

"Who's that?"

"Barry!"

"Oh, lover man!" Her voice was suddenly more alive; interested.

"Called off for lunch today with Blacky," he said, wanting to get directly to the point of the conversation. He didn't feel like talking. He didn't feel like anything, but maybe laying *down* and dying.

"Oh." She sounded almost relieved, or was that his imagination? "Sorry."

"So am I. Make it for later?" He thought that over and quickly added. "Maybe, tonight?—No! Let me call you after I see Blacky. Who knows, this might be an assignment. And it would be just breaking another date."

* * * * * * *

Joan didn't know if she felt regret about the broken engagement or not. It was a series of jagged incomplete thoughts and emotions that flashed through her.

Barry: that loving man who connected with her body in such a tender-violent way. How she wanted him; forever!

It was silly and childish to think she was in love with Barry. On the other hand, why did she feel anything?

Slowly she put the receiver back on the hook. Slowly, without even knowing she was doing it.

Last night had troubled her.

Barry's reaction concerning Ann Cummings was starkly naked. The man was totally taken by the other women! Apparently they had met and he'd been captured by that raw, open innocence, that caring gentle woman the blonde truly was. Intelligent, soft, loving—and lost in a dirty living trap.

The fury that had twisted about in her head as she watched the expressions move across Barry's face had left her without much interest in what had followed.

Now those same little torments seemed to be rubbing in

through the pores of her skin.

She had told him the blunt truth about herself and Ann. She had felt as if she were controlled by another person. As if what she said and did were enacted by an outsider. She couldn't stop. There was that part of her enjoying every moment, every delicious revelation about Ann, the lovely, blonde mistress of Blacky Jenson. Any serious thoughts about the woman would be blasted away by such information. No man, certainly, could love a woman who turned herself into one of Blacky's personal whores. And this part of her wanted to crush any possible interest Barry might have to the other woman.

At that same time, the better part of herself wondered if this might be Ann's last chance to escape from the hell of this life—before it was too late for her. It was too late for Joan Verril. She had gone too far down the tubes. But Ann Cummings still had a chance—and at least a chance was better than being trapped for life.

Yet…Joan felt a flush of evil joy at telling him the raw truth. Let him stew in that reality. Maybe that would leave him open to continuing to be with…

Joan the tramp…the whore…slut…drunk.

She hated that part of herself. She wanted to remember the better side, the caring part, the part that literally felt something strangely powerful, overwhelming, even if insane, for Barry. If it was love it was bordering on selfish love. Not the kind that would willingly share or release…

She broke those thoughts away. She shattered them from her mind.

Angrily she started dressing. Another day. Another instant in her life that would just repeat what had been before. It was like a record that was on the top of the stack which just kept playing over and over, until the melody, the musical line, had stopped meaning anything.

She pulled on the bra and felt the soft texture of the cloth against her flesh. A swelling thrill waved through her. The cloth felt almost like a tender caress of Barry's hands.

Oh, she thought, *he is good!*

Not like other men.

Joan sighed, partly sick, partly thrilled in the memory of

90

this man; the only one she really remembered having treated her with any kind of respect. Barry loved in a way that proved he cared; considering her another human being.

Nobody else cared about anything but poking her. No matter if she was ready or not.

She'd have to call Ann and tell her the news—unless the girl knew already.

The poor thing. Frightened to death. Scared. And wanting out. Get out. Away from Blacky Jenson. His craving passions. He wasn't much of a lover; not much of a man. Just a bastard with a lot of power over those who came into his web of hell.

Ann deserved better. There was still something in this girl that could be saved, if given the chance. In that way she was better than Joan. She could be rescued, pulled away from the whole thing with a part of her good side still intact.

Maybe if Barry helped her escape. Maybe then they would find happiness. Maybe the two of them fit.

She shrugged her shoulders. Her gut felt ill at the thought of Ann and Barry. The idea of any other woman with Barry was horrible. It made her... *This was just plain foolish!*

Maybe someone should do something about Blacky. Ann, Barry, herself—and every other person in the damn world.

* * * * * * *

"Okay, here's the deal!" Blacky Jenson explained, tapping his big cigar against the edge of the small glass ashtray. His eyes were cold ice, his face frozen emotion.

He was a dangerous man.

Barry knew that. He had realized it before. But since yesterday he'd learned one hell of a lot about the man, and discovered a deep hate welling inside him.

It was difficult not to push the man's face in a foot or two. Crush it into a pulp. But far too dangerous.

He hadn't liked the man from the beginning. Now he despised his guts.

Because of the business he was in. Selling young girls to

the highest bidder. Because of Joan, for what he had made of her. And most of all, because of Ann. For what he was doing to her.

But business was business. He needed money. One more job, and he would pull out. And maybe the rug out from under Blacky.

At first he had thought to make himself a little stock pile. Build up a large bank account. When he had been contacted by Jenson's men in New York the week before, dollar signs had clicked in his brain.

Now, it was different.

Make the money to get Nelly out of hock, and then off to the wild blue yonder.

"Our contact man in Boise," Blacky continued, looking meaningfully at Barry, and then turning to Benton, "has gotten a few jobs. All lined up at once. You know the kind, Denny, about a week's work. You take up a load of girls, drop them, Benton stays, and you, Davis, fly back. You can pick up the sex-cargo next week when the work is finished. Okay? Get it?"

Barry nodded.

It was a lousy day. Hot and cloudy. The hangover was almost gone, but not the nausea. It couldn't leave while Jenson was within screaming distance of him.

"You go this afternoon, around four or five. How's that fit your schedule?" Blacky asked Barry, pointing at him with his cigar.

"Fine."

"Good." The man stood, and Benton followed his example. "I wish you a good trip, men."

He shook hands with both of them and left the restaurant.

Barry ordered another drink, looked across at Hawky and wanted to smash the man's face in two.

He'd had his stomach filled. Completely. All the way up. And any moment, hour, or day he was going to vomit it out. Out right in the face of these slobs who made money the dirty way.

Right down your face too, Hawky.

His eyes met those of the other man and he saw an odd

light in them. The guy was looking at Barry as if trying to size him up; make his mind up about something. Finally he slowly killed the cigarette butt he'd been smoking and then after lighting another one and blowing smoke into the air, his eyes met Barry's again. "You don't like Blacky, do you?"

"How'd you guess?"

"Just say that I know how people are. Get to know— sometimes..." A silly grin spread across his thin lips, as he tapped his jaw slightly. "Except with you, buddy. Still sore!"

Good! Good for good old Hawky's sore jaw!

Another silence. They smoked for awhile, waiting for the drinks. Benton was about to talk again when the cocktail girl came. Once they were alone once more, he leaned forward. "Maybe I shouldn't tell you or say anything about it ... but..."

What?

"What the hell are you talking about?"

He couldn't care less.

"You're a right guy! I gotta hand it to you," Benton continued, leaning even closer, after having looked around to see that nobody was within hearing distance. "Gotta respect a guy who doesn't take any pushing around. So, I'll give it to you straight!" Another pause. They stared at each other for a long time. "Get out after this job!"

That one hit hard. He hadn't known what to expect—but certainly not this. "Why?"

"Just do as I say—and you won't get hurt!" What the hell! He saw it now. The guy was afraid of him. Scared that maybe Barry was about to take *his* place in the organization. "Look, I don't like being threatened! I thought you understood that!"

Surprise showed in the other's eyes. "Isn't that at all! You got me all wrong!"

"Sure. Sure I do!" Barry started to stand and leave.

"Wait! You don't understand at all!"

He turned and looked down at Hawk-Face. The emotion in the man's voice had gotten to him. The guy looked like he really was trying to tell him something. What?

"Look—*spit it out!*"

There was a pause and then Benton motioned him to sit

down. After he had done so, the man leaned close again and whispered, "The boom is about to be lowered by the big boys upstairs. They don't like the way Blacky is shaping up and getting out of hand. They see him as a threat."

That one froze his insides. That's all he needed to do, get in the middle of a gang-war. Pictures of the Prohibition days flashed before his mind. Valentine's Day!

"You...you're kidding!" he whispered weakly, hoping the guy was giving him the needle—or a test! *Testing him?*

"What makes you think I won't go and tell Blacky. Warn him. Say that you've been playing dirty-pool on him. Double-crossing him?"

"I'd just laugh and say it was all a lie."

"Then why are you telling me all this? What's in it for you?"

"Nothing, buddy. Just trying to warn you. Everybody else is in on it. Some are pulling out after this next job—for good. Others are getting ready to go on over to the organization." He put out his cigarette. "Look, I'm on the level. Don't know why—except, maybe I don't like to see a guy with guts get a raw deal. At least, not in the back. Not knowing how the score is lining up."

Thanks, Buddy, old pal!

"What's the word? When do the big boys send their big bad killers to wipe the bunch of us out?" he asked, still not quite convinced that the man wasn't kidding or testing him for Blacky.

Benton laughed. It was a sputtering sound.

Barry knew then that it had been all a joke. He knew, and wanted to beat the guy into a pulpy mass of flesh, blood and bone. Lay his guts wide open.

Then Hawky sobered. "You've been seeing too much television. They don't work that way no more. Nowadays, all they do is give someone in the D.A.'s office a hot tip and the law does the work for them. Closes in real nice. Everybody lands in jail and then another group is sent in to carry!" He started to stand. "So, like I tell you. If you know what's good for you, you'll pull out while the getting's good."

Then the man was gone, leaving Barry quite dazed and bewildered. What the guy had told him was enough to upset anybody. But the very fact that he *had* told him was worse; that really bugged him.

Finally he shrugged and stood. *Some guys will worship someone who's given them a beating.*

Yet, maybe it was just a little test to see just how far he could be trusted.

He didn't know really what to think.

But that didn't really change a thing. He was already planning on getting out, fast.

Chapter *ELEVEN*

Two days without Barry.

Two days to wait. Wonder. Hate.

That was her trouble. She was beginning to hate too much. Hate Jenson. Hate Wilmore. Hate men. Hate life. It was a killing germ inside that sliced at her body and mind. It was an angry ache that wouldn't stop.

Over and over.

Two days of misery. And no word, Just a phone call saying to call off the date with Ann.

Break the engagement.

It had been hard telling the girl it was off. But that wasn't so important, really.

Just a phone call. "Darling—I'm sorry, but Barry can't make it!" Simple. But somehow she felt bad about it. Yet, in another way she was glad. Every moment she kept the two of them apart, she had Barry a little longer for herself. For she knew once he and Ann made the connections she would be the third party.

Neither had said it. They didn't have to. She knew it as well as if told in so many words.

"I love Barry."

"I love Ann."

She didn't think they realized it themselves. But people were strange creatures. They spoke with their actions, their reactions. They told the simple truths in the way they looked, the way they didn't do something that should be done. The way Barry's hand had slipped from hers when she mentioned Ann to him.

That told her too much.

They were in love. And hardly knew each other. They each had something the other wanted; the other needed.

96

And the sad thing was that Barry had something that she needed. Joan needed him because he was good. The only good thing she knew. The only thing that really counted.

That was strange. *She* hardly knew Barry. A few passion nights. That was all there was between them. But he had filled a desperate longing in her. He had been tender. Kind. Passionate but gentle. A gentleness which he didn't even know he expressed. An action that was as normal for him, as brute force was normal to men like Blacky Jenson and Wilmore.

Poor Willy didn't mean to be cruel. He just didn't know anything else. He just used a girl, banging his fat prick at her as if she were some machine.

Blacky was different. He knew something else. It was just that he *liked* being cruel. He *liked* the brute force. He enjoyed taking virgins and making sluts and whores out of them. He liked ruining other people's lives—because that gave his life meaning in his eyes. Made him powerful; God-like in his mind.

He liked getting people started on dope. Because that meant more money in his pocket.

He'd tried dope on her; but that was where she drew the line.

He took the creative power in himself, and used it to destroy. And someone some day would feed that force right to him. It would circle back, like it only could circle back. Once you put an action into circulation, that same action would return to you in doubled or tripled force. It was the nature of the universe. You can't start something without getting the automatic results.

And she *sure* got them.

But it wasn't really her fault.

Blacky had made her into what she was. And what she was, just wasn't nice. An alcoholic and oversexed female. Her body was just one raging desire after another. She couldn't help that. Any more than she could help breathing.

But someday she would be just plain tired. Tired of the whole thing. And she knew that would be soon.

The phone at her desk rang. She picked it up.

"Wilmore here!" the voice said.

Willy—the pill!

Yet, even he wasn't so bad. He had a lot of the same hungers she possessed. Being that type of man, he couldn't channel them into a finer action like Barry's. Barry was sensitive. Willy felt an urge and reacted in the most direct, automatic fashion he was capable of offering up.

"Hello. How is it, darling?" she asked, more interested than she thought possible. After all, she reasoned, maybe she could get him to come around that evening. It might be a good outlet.

A good...

She was almost anxious about the idea. He was her kind. Her kind of person, even more than Barry. He was physical. Animal. And in reality, Joan made herself admit, she was *exactly* like him in that way.

Too much exactly!

* * * * * * *

For Barry it was a nonstop flight. From beginning to end, with a short pause at Boise. After that, he just started up the engines after refueling and took off for Los Angeles.

He was tired when he got back to his apartment. Dead tired. Too tired to drink. Too tired to eat. And too tired to call up any woman.

Even Joan.

He slept twenty-four hours, and for the first time in days felt rested and fresh in the morning. Almost felt it was nice to be alive.

No hangover. No problems.

To speak of.

Alive and ready to go.

Where?

He remembered Ann, and the appointment he had been forced to miss because of Jenson.

He remembered Joan, who could arrange a meeting with the two of them.

He called Joan's apartment. No answer. He called her at work. She wasn't in.

With disgust he dressed, went down to the hotel coffee

shop and had breakfast.

A cute brunette waited on him. She was pert and pixy looking. Her tiny figure displayed several delicate curves. But nothing like Joan—or Ann for that matter. A casual urge ran through him. She looked like the kind that would willingly play bedroom games, if given the chance. The way she smiled as she took his order. The seductive way she leaned across the counter so that he could just barely see the slight opening at the top of her uniform. He couldn't see much. But what little he did see, seemed damn little. Small tiny knots, firm—yet interesting.

There was little doubt that he could have her by simply snapping his fingers. She was probably no better than so many whores or tramps; and he'd known a lot.

But a whore was a whore. Just a body to sink himself into. And that's the way this girl seemed; young, tiny, but all-too eager. She might be good. But she would be just as whorish as so many others he'd known.

Except, he remembered, *there were some exceptions!*

Once he'd been with a Mexican whore, in Mexico City. The woman had a great body and couldn't have been over eighteen, at most; and she looked younger.

In a way this cute little waitress reminded him of that prostitute; maybe because they both seemed far younger looking than they were. And if he'd learned anything about life from the Mexican whore, it had been you couldn't tell what a girl was like until you were in bed with them.

Yes, he thought, he'd known some real whores. But none of them had been like Joan; and now his taste for such carnal sex was best satisfied by her lush, passionate body.

If he had to screw somebody, he decided let it be Joan's; he could wait. For of all the sex-pots he'd known in life, Joan was probably the best lushing tramp in bed.

Barry even hated thinking of Joan in that way, because he couldn't help responding to her as a person. It was the difference in her attitude and something about the woman herself that could touch a man—if he'd let it happen.

It was hardly worth it.

So, Barry could ignore the waitress. He only vaguely wondered what he life must be line; was she a single mom?

Had she been used by some man in the past? Was she simply lone? A sad story, no doubt.

Still, he bet she drew in a lot of male customers for breakfast, lunch and dinner. The coffee-break girl. And the quickie mid-night lay.

It was a lazy morning and nothing seemed to be moving in any direction. Nothing to do.

He didn't feel like a drink. There had been enough boozing it up in the last few days to take care of him for awhile. He normally wasn't a heavy drinker. But things had moved in on him pretty fast.

The party. Joan throwing herself at him. He wondered if Blacky had told her to do it. He might have. The meeting of Ann. The hot job that night with Joan. And then seeing Ann the next day. The kiss. The emotions welling through him until he could hardly think. React. Understand...The trip to Frisco. The two whores. He couldn't remember much about that night.

Scotch and 151 *Rum!*

That one made him laugh. No wonder he hadn't remembered anything. That had been a bomb.

Then Joan again. A fiery exchange of hungry passions. Then the jolt! The announcement that the blonde innocence, which had been plaguing his every thought, wanted to arrange a meeting with him. Wanted to see him.

Everything happening so fast.

Too fast!

This was the first time he had been able to think about it. The first time he was able to realize what was happening. The first time he was mentally relaxed enough to think straight. And the conclusions were fantastic.

Love!

He just wasn't that kind of man. Yet, that was what was happening. It *must* be the reason he felt like he did.

Love?

That was the word created by the story book romanticists. It was a state-of-mind that you could fall into anytime you wanted.

He could fall in love with Joan. It wouldn't mean anything. Like the turning on and off of a water faucet. Nothing more emotional.

Then turn it off, copper-brain! Turn it off!

He couldn't.

He couldn't get Ann out of his mind. He wanted her. He wanted to feel her form against him again. He wanted to put his arms around her, and take her away from the ugly world she lived in. He wanted to pull her out of that trap.

A trap of fear.

Passionate lusts.

Or moral degeneration.

Before she became another Joan. Before she was just another one of the girls.

He wanted to protect her. Take care of her.

Stop it!

Stop!

He stood, called the waitress over, asked for the bill. Paid it. And walked out. He had to do something. Anything. But he had to stop thinking—tick-tick! Slow the little machine down to a complete vacation before there was a breakdown from over work!

Maybe old Nelly would help. Maybe a shot in the sky would take the pressures off. Maybe.

Always maybe.

* * * * * * *

Joan woke up with a dry ugly taste in her mouth. Dry and heavy with the leftover sense of sex.

She went into the living room, picked up the all but empty bottle, poured herself a drink, then another. That helped a little to blot out the memory of the sexual session with Willy.

She felt over her body. It ached. Her breasts were bruised and her lips felt sore.

It had been sick sex of the most perverted kind.

Willy had told her to strip, the minute they were alone together.

He was a beast.

The only thing she'd experienced was a sick sense of having been carnally taken, like an animal to be used without

101

any considerations concerning her own feelings.

It was the long session with Willy.

Thankfully, Willy had left afterwards and she had drunk herself to unconsciousness, thinking about Barry and how wonderful it was with him. How different!

In a way she had to thank Willy for *one* thing. It had been blunt, steel-like hammering of a man's body against hers. She had been able to get lost in her passions; forget, just for the moment, and the wanting that was inspired by Barry. He was the only man who had inspired thoughts of love; the longing to be married, bear children. Willy had made it possible to become a beast of passion that didn't think.

She would be glad when Barry got back.

She shivered.

She didn't want to be in love. She didn't like the idea of getting emotionally attached. She didn't like it—but there was nothing she could do about it. Barry had sparked something very real within her that was more than mere orgasm.

And it would not last. It would end, soon. And there wasn't anything she could do about that.

Ann Cummings.

She'd have to make the arrangements. Again. They'd have to get together. There was no question about it.

They would get together, and then she would be out of Barry's life—before she had even been given a chance to get in; she'd be history.

Chapter *TWELVE*

When Barry approached Nelly, he had no idea what he was to find inside of private territory. He could never have guessed what awaited him.

As he slipped into the plane, he was hardly aware of anything starting for the pilot's compartment. It was then that he became aware that somebody else was there.

Barry was stunned to see her. He just hadn't expected it. Especially after what Joan had told him. That it would be better for Ann to meet him in secret. That she was afraid that someone might see them together, and questions would be asked as a result.

So it was a jolt.

But there she was. Blonde hair falling over her shoulders. Her long willowy body stretched out in one of the seats of the passenger cabin. She was asleep. Her breathing was light, but the rise and fall of her breasts showed through the loose-fitting white blouse she wore.

He found it hard not to lean over and touch her. To kiss those large yet delicate lips. He wanted to.

Instead he coughed. It was a loud, awkward sound. Unnatural. Yet it served its purpose.

Her eyes opened. Blue as skies. Bright and shinning. Alert. With that incredible innocence.

Little Miss Innocence.

He didn't like that last thought. Not at all. Not in the least. He shook it out of his mind. Refused to think of her as anything except what she appeared to be. A nice young girl from the country who hadn't been touched by the filth of civilization. The dirt of city life. Still having that untouched look. A pure virgin. Clean. That's what he saw. That's what she looked like. Childlike. And that was what he would be-

103

lieve. Had to make himself believe.

Damn it! What was wrong with him, it didn't really make any difference. Why did he care what she was? All that should matter to him was that she was a woman he wanted, and he would take her, if he got the chance.

Without realizing it, he had tensed all over. Every muscle was hard and rigid.

She looked up at him, a frown touching her features. Then she smiled. Her lips spreading warm and glistening across even white teeth. Raising her arms above her head she stretched sleepily, her body shivering slightly. Her breasts surging outwards, pointed and larger looking than he had thought they might be. She had a delicate frame, but the curves were there, neat and compact. Not as voluptuous as Joan's, not as animal-like, but completely adequate.

Perfectly adequate.

Just perfect!

A sigh sounded from her as she stood.

"I'm sorry, I fell asleep," she apologized.

He shrugged. He was lost as to what to say. He wasn't quite sure what was expected of him. Not quite sure how to handle the situation.

They stood looking at each other for a long time. Silence. Quiet and heavy. For the first time since they had seen each other that night at Blacky Jenson's party, they seemed strangers.

Strangers who had never met before.

Strangers that had nothing in common.

And he realized just how much that role fit them. They *didn't* know each other. They had only spoken twice before.

They *were* strangers.

Yet, he had felt something different before. As if they knew everything about each other. That they were very much the same underneath.

Maybe everybody was fairly much the same. Everybody had to be needed and loved. Everybody desired fulfillment of their passions, their ambitions, their lives. In a way the human race was just billions of little reproductions of the same things. The same being. The same motivations. You saw in others what you wanted to see. He saw innocence in Ann. He

104

saw cruel passion, lusts, and failure in Joan. Yet all three of them were much the same person. All three wanted something better, and all three were trapped in their own little lives, unable to get out, unable to escape.

No, he didn't know Ann, any more than he knew himself. Or any less than he knew his best friend. Each person was an island that only repeated the same problems existing in the other islands surrounding them. The only difference was the outer appearance of those problems, and the way persons went about solving them. And the way others saw them.

He knew Ann, and knew her because she was so very much like himself. He didn't have to have known her for days, months or years. Like with Joan he understood. And to understand was to know. He knew Ann, and in a way maybe loved her. Loved her because he saw what he wanted in her. He saw the good, instead of the bad.

The *bad* was just a mistake.

Like Joan. Joan wasn't really what she looked like. On the surface she was a little tramp. Physical and passionate. A slut.

On the surface Ann was innocent, clean and good. Bright sunshine. But caught in her own little trap. A trap brought about by a little two-bit hood. A vise that clamped down on her life and held her. Even beyond her control to get free.

He didn't know how long they stood there, thinking and wondering, questioning and desiring.

He knew that he wasn't interested in *what* Ann was. He wasn't interested in anything but what he *saw* in her. What he wanted to see in her. The mistakes could be cut out, and forgotten. And after that, there would only be the true person. The person reflected and revealed in her eyes. All the mistakes, experiences of a lifetime had made her into the woman she now was, the woman there before him.

Then suddenly he realized that he had reached out, pulled her into his arms. The shock of holding her, so impulsively and boldly moved, and finding her willingly clutching so firmly to him, was overpowering.

The loveliness of her, the soft, graceful, yet beautifully

sensual pressure of this woman's form molding itself against his like a lover's, created such a swelling wave of pleasure to flood through him that Barry felt dizzy.

He realized she was trembling, all over. Then he became aware of soft sobs. It was as if he were holding a child-like mature woman who had turned to him, longingly, crying on his shoulder. And because of that she didn't seem like a stranger any more, but rather a deep, dear part of him.

He could hardly believe what he was thinking. Yet, regardless, it was obviously the kind of emotion a man felt toward a woman he loved.

He wasn't getting hooked up with any broad! Not Barry Davis! His mind screamed both in panic and surprise.

For only a short moment they were moved by this wild tender emotion. Then something took place, maybe the awareness of their bodies so tightly together; the normal animal instincts of the flesh taking over. The very smell of her excited him. The delightful feel of that soft, tiny body next to his was overpowering.

He gently raised her lips and covered them with his own. Then desperation raced their actions. The animal need took control. An emotion that burst up over them from their very souls and minds as well as from their guts.

He knew her thigh was pressing insistently between his legs.

He hadn't felt this way since he was a kid, in the middle of his first childhood crush. It was more than the passion to take, invade her body. He wanted much more than that; he wanted to love and protect her, possess all that was this woman.

And he realized he was in love.

Just like that, without any qualifications.

He was crushed downwards into the well of his own mind. A pit that seemed to crumble his own false ideals, his own false beliefs, and destroy them. And he had never been so happy in his whole life.

Then the pleasure of her body pressing urgently against his sparked the physical urge into a roaring fire. An electric power twisted through every part of his being like an insane torrent. It was a flooding wild surge of pleasure and strength that seemed endless—making him sure there wasn't any problem in the world that he couldn't solve, as long as he could have Ann in his arms, loving her.

The tenderness of their first embrace melted into tense passion; and they weren't trying to be spiritual or emotional. It was a man and woman, maturely needing one another in every way; but in a form that would consume their bodies in white heat. A passion that was almost spiritual—touching *all* their emotions.

Her lips parted wildly and her body writhed up hard against his, her thigh convulsively moving back and forth, thrillingly caressing.

Now she wanted to be taken, fully, giving of herself, in every way, and most of all, in the most intimate manner possible.

A gift and act of love.

Her tongue probed gently into his mouth, searching, lingering as if tasting wine, then he was thrilling to this taste of her mouth, as their bodies seemed to blend even tighter together.

This wasn't the kind of sexual escape he had experienced with all too many women. This was what life could be all about; something to make living worth while.

Then their kiss parted, they pressed their cheeks together and Ann moaned: "I've never felt like this before in all my life. I've never wanted to *give* myself to a man like I want to give myself to you."

They looked lovingly, longingly into one another's eyes and there was no question about what would happen next. There was no escaping the total union of their bodies in a complete act of love.

* * * * * * *

Joan was tired when she arrived home from work that evening. The second day she hadn't seen Barry.

She poured a drink and slowly began sipping it.

There was little doubt in her mind now as to her feelings toward Barry. There could be little room for any other belief than that she was in love with him. Hardly knowing him.

And falling in love with a stranger. But that was life.

The phone rang. She moved over to it and picked up the receiver, hoping that it would be Barry. Her body warmed at the thought. The blood raced through her excitedly.

"Hello?" she sighed, anxiously waiting for the sound of his voice.

It must be him! Had to be!

"Hello, baby-doll, this is Blacky," the gruff, grating voice came over the receiver.

That jolted her in two ways; it *wasn't* Barry, it *was* Blacky.

She had hardly expected to hear from him. It made her feel a cold ice-knot in her guts. *She hated him.! Oh, how she hated him!*

"I'm planning a party for next Saturday, Joan, I wonder—"

"What's the bit?"

"Flight to Boise to pick up some of the girls. Thought it would be a good chance to get to know the flyboy better. You know...give him another watch with a woman. Like to see a man enjoying himself—might be interesting! Thought you'd like to come along."

She didn't have to think long to know she liked the idea. A whole weekend caught up with Barry.

"I'm taking Ann along, and you could pair off with Davis. If you don't mind any..." The voice wasn't asking. It was telling. The man had good reasons in the back of his mind. She didn't know what. But she had never seen Blacky do anything without good reason. Maybe it would be smart to play along.

She felt cold all of a sudden. Desperately cold. But she'd have to warn Barry. Warn him to be on his guard.

Chapter *THIRTEEN*

As Barry watched Ann Cummings walk across the airstrip, he felt as if an important part of himself were leaving. A part of the childlike romantic.

Never had a woman given such pleasure. Never had any been so wonderful. It wasn't just her actions; her passion; her kiss; her fiery body. It was something else, something that radiated from within her and bathed him in its luminescence. Passion was passion. A body was a body—*yet Ann had made it all seem different.*

There was that quality about her that was all the difference in the world. And there could be no question now as to the way he felt about her. It wasn't what he had planned to let happen. But then, life never worked out the way it was planned. He was in love with her, and felt sure she returned it. That was the way it had worked. That's the way it had turned out.

Three short meetings and they were in love.

He had never believed in love at first sight. And he still didn't. Maybe they were in a trap of their own making. Ann wanting to get away, out, escape, and seeing it in him and his plane. Barry wanting her as a woman, and then slowly finding himself entrapped in a new staked pit. No matter how he struggled, he couldn't get away. He could not get out. She had him pinned down and finished for sure. And she knew it.

There had been no words once the mutual agreement had been made in their silent glance. Nothing but the boiling desires were suddenly set free. The desperate urges flooding outwards, taking over their bodies. It was explosive, dynamite.

His hands, caressing, undressed her. They loved her breasts with tenderness while she helped him remove his

109

clothing. He loved her thighs, face. He loved every inch of her flesh with his eyes and hands.

Then they were naked, their bodies pressed tightly together. There wasn't anything vulgar in their love-making. Not even as she had lowered his pants down, lovingly kissed him with silken lips in a worshipping act of total giving.

But now, holding her to him, feeling the warmth of her thrilling to the pressure of her soft supple breasts as they cushioned against his chest, kissing first her lips then cheeks, then eyes and nose, forehead, neck, throat, hearing her moans of soft pleasure, feeling her hands caressing his back, running along his spine, lovingly, all so loving.

Every other woman in his life faded to meaningless physical acts.

This was special. Ann was love itself.

Then he held his hand behind her head, tongued her lips, felt her tongue against the tip of his—then she tensed all over, her body writhed, giving him a love-caress all over. His own hands moved gently over her body, against her soft, yielding breasts, palming her nipples until they were hardened points. Then he made love to her breasts, kissing them in an emotional way he had never done with any woman; lightly moving his tongue around their points, over their fleshy, delicate surface, then pulling one nipple ever-so gently between his lips, letting his tongue touch, caress the end.

She surged up against his erotic kiss. Every action she made was that of an experienced female, yet so totally different, filling her touch with emotion that reached deeply within him like a flood of overwhelming love.

It seemed as if there had been an endless black hole inside his total being which was now overflowing with the wonder of this woman who generously enveloped his total being in something so complete that it left no room for anything other than all that was her.

His hands glided down to the rounded curve of her hip and she automatically parted her thighs. That one act actually sparked the fire beyond control.

She grabbed at his shoulders, her thighs parted wider and suddenly he was in the depths of her body, wildly aware of nothing other than being within the warm embrace of the

110

wonderful woman's very soul. It was more than a sexual en-
velop that swallow him whole; it was a blending of all that
they were, had ever been and could ever be. She clutched
upwards so that their bodies were fully touching. Then their
hips moved and he felt the slow driving wildness building to
a complete need of their bodies to move as one, to be one, to
float in an endless ecstasy.

Yet it lasted.

He felt her climax, then experienced his own first voluptuous swell of ecstasy, yet couldn't leave the wonderful
warmth of her depths. Their lips moved against one another,
merely swaying back and forth. Her legs kept him in a gentle
embrace, ankles hooked around his calves, making it all too
obvious that she didn't want him to leave her; not yet. Or
maybe never.

They kissed, lovingly, lips closed. It was the kind of
lover's kiss that meant more than mere passion; it was the act
of two people saying silently how much they had received
and were still enjoying. How needy they were just for one
another, for each other, for this union which had been fused
in such wild, wonderful, loving passion. Their bodies had
mated and their souls had blended into one total being.

Then she moved her hips so that he was caressed within
the confines of her, making him aware that he was still in
almost full erection. The movement surged quick fire
through him and they were again stroking one another in the
total intimacy of physical union; and with each gentle thrust
the passion built, lasting only a little longer, because the
hungers for one another had been built to such a great need
that only total fiery rhythm could momentarily consume the
surface heat. When he climaxed again, her body joined his in
the final ecstasy. It was like a mutual concerto of endless
sound, sensation, and an eternal blessing that drown them
into a fusion of total oneness.

And though in reality everything had been much the
same as with any other woman—the actions, the sounds, the
smells, the tastes, the terrible anguished burn—it had been
all different.

It was an instant of eternity that flashed explosively like
a huge big bang, creating a totally new universe to expand

around their inner beings. All that had been was simply washed away into a distant, meaningless past, and now they were in a new dimension, a new universe, and a reborn universe where anything was possible. In that state they floated in ecstatic joy. A forever moment that simply couldn't last long enough.

And over far too soon.

As they shot through the height of their lovely overwhelming last ecstatic ecstasy together and then slowly floated back to reality, he knew there would never be any experience to match this with another woman. With Ann it could only get better, more beautiful; more perfect. A perfection which would be self-inventing into a new, brighter, richer perfection. Evolving endless through eternity.

Illusion, yet the only reality he ever wanted to have in his life. Without her, without this, nothing else counted. All else, in fact, was suddenly shallow, dull, flat: meaningless.

They talked then. They could talk then. Before it would have been impossible. Insane. Filled with torment. Desire.

Now they talked. And the questions welled up in him, controlling his lips, sending the words out into the air one after another.

How? Why?

He wanted to know how she happened to be there? Why she had come? And why not before? Why she had run before. Some of the answers he knew. He guessed. He hoped. But he had to hear them from her own lips, her own heart.

"I...I couldn't wait. When Joan told me that you wouldn't be able to make it for the lunch the other day...I didn't know what I'd do. From that first night there had been something which drew us—compelled us—together. I mean—*this had to happen!* Sometime."

He stroked her hair gently, trying to soothe understanding, love, and calmness in her.

"I—had to see you. We had...the afternoon when you first came out here—I'd..." A guilty, shy smile worked the corner of her lips upwards. "I knew about you. I mean, I planned to meet...see you here...But the kiss. The emotions were too...I was afraid."

Silence.

112

Suddenly everything had been said. He understood. He knew what they must do now. Some way, somehow they would find a way to be together—*to escape!*

Now they talked about other things. Of nothing of importance. And then everything. Their childhood. Their plans. The future together.

Smoking during the silences, when they just sat close to each other, feeling the nearness; the awareness, they seemed to be drawn even closer together—physically, emotionally, and mentally.

"What are we going to do about..." he couldn't mention the man's name. He couldn't talk about anybody who might have touched, caressed, kissed and taken her, as he had just taken her.

No. Nobody had ever had her the way she had just given herself to him. He knew that so deeply within him that nothing else mattered. Past history was gone! Only now and the future counted; had meaning. With her.

Yet, here he couldn't mention Blacky Jenson's name. He didn't dare even think of the man who had been responsible for her getting a beating which had landed her in the hospital. For that, Barry would kill Jenson, before the whole thing was finished. He would kill him with his bare hands, beating the life out of the fat big-shot. Letting him die slowly.

Ann shook her head gently, and her soft blonde hair brushed his cheek. Then she said: "I have to get away from him. Somehow."

Tears clouded her eyes.

He knew what she meant. They had to find a way. They would find one—*somehow.*

Her head nestled down on his shoulder and they sat for a long while. Each thinking hard, each trying to find a way out.

"Another country?" he suggested. "We could take the plane up and fly to Mexico or Canada, South America, anywhere!"

She shrugged. "He has contacts in Mexico, through his dope smuggling. We wouldn't be safe anywhere. Not with the big business operations he's connected with. Even though he's just a small-fry as far as the all-over *organization* is concerned."

"Didn't know he was in the dope line." Barry felt a tenseness of frosted surprise run through him. He remembered what Benton had told him the other day about the *organization* getting ready to close down Blacky Jenson's operations. Maybe that had been the straight scoop.

"Blacky's a real nasty man. In a little of everything. Numbers racket, race track, political machine—just about everything. You'd have been brought into the whole thing after awhile. Once he has you hooked real good with the call girl thing. He needs men to smuggle things across the border. Things like dope, whore, you name it. Even wetbacks. Once he has his thumb on a man—or woman—and is sure of them, he lets you in, but good! Then there's no stopping. You're sucked into the chain-gang and you can't get out.

"I tried to warn you that first evening. He's a dirty little man! Even for his bloated size!" A bitter laugh ran through her then, and he felt the responding action as she shook against him. It reminded him of their nearness, their nakedness, and their warmth.

He turned around and kissed her. The soft give of her lips parted under his and he felt a moistness reach out eagerly.

For a long moment they held close, each frantically exploiting the excitement of the other. Tense. Their bodies hardened by the violence which suddenly took control of every muscle and nerve. Then they relaxed, breathing hard.

He could feel her breasts moving against his chest, the soft, supple flesh pumping like firm velvet spheres. A need ran through him.

Finally the weak-happiness calmed down, and the contentment of knowing the wants and demands of the other reflected in themselves was enough—perfect and wonderful.

"We'll think of something," he told her, tenderly caressing her. "Somehow we'll get you out of this...get us both out—for good!"

Then abruptly they were kissing and touching and moving tightly together.

Like two people with one mind, they both knew when

114

the other was ready for the other.

It was slow and gentle, this time, both of their bodies moving, circling against one another in even, controlled movements. Both of them were looking at one another and it was a strange experience, for he could almost hear her words, silently spoken. He could read the thoughts of pleasure, the caressing statements love in her gaze.

That love totally enveloped him, sounding, and mingling, surging into and becoming one with his own overwhelming love for her.

Then she suddenly held her arms out and folded them about his neck. They kissed gently, then continued to gaze into one another's eyes as the erotic moments of their hips took on a more insistent rhythm, building the pleasure, creating voluptuous sensations to electrify them. He could almost feel her own ecstasy as sharply as his. Never once did they stop gazing into one another's eyes even as the climatic moments of ecstasy waved over them again and again like flooding waters rising and falling.

It seemed as if they simply joined in an electric fusion.

They continued to hold one another for some time. Then parted for what might have been moments or hours, not speaking in words, only in the warmth of their glances, as if their souls were connected, as if their thoughts were one.

Then, later, she was gone and Barry had never felt so alone in his private hell.

Chapter *FOURTEEN*

Joan thought Barry would never call. It seemed as if he had been gone for years. Yet only two days had passed.

But now more depended on his getting in touch with her than just her own desires, her own desperate urge to be with him and see him and feeling alive. It was because of this new, more dangerous element that she became frantic. She tried getting hold of him at his hotel, but they said he was out. After that, she didn't know where to look next. The airstrip on Blacky's country home would be the logical place. But she didn't dare try calling out there.

So she just had to wait.

She tried working. But that didn't do much good, for her mind couldn't keep on what she was doing. Finally she gave up, cancelled all appointments and went home.

There she started drinking. Drinking until the suffering twisted away from her insides. Until her mind was so light and airy that thoughts just seemed to float away into nothingness. She knew how to drink to a certain, ideal, point where it was possible to avoid going over the "line" and out of it completely.

Then the phone rang.

Her heart stopped beating. Then it speeded up. Wildly pumping the blood through her. She shivered, then felt a surging burn run over her.

"Hello?" she cried, much too loud. Much too excited.

"Hello, Joan?"

It was Barry! She was happy all over. Warm and cold all at once.

"Hi. Been quite a spell!" she said calmly, forcing her voice to keep from shaking from excitement.

"Yeah. Heard you were trying to get hold of me."

116

"Had to see you. Something important."

"Doing anything tonight?"

"No," she blurted out. *Oh, no, nothing that would ever get in the way of the two of us being together!*

"Then I'll be over in a little while."

She hung up. Poured herself another drink, downed it, and sat in a chair.

Slowly the liquor moved through her nervous system, and time seemed to slide past with a delightful speed.

After all, a girl like herself—a lush—was lucky to know a real man like Barry, if only for a few moments out of his life. That, alone, was worth the price of admission—and she'd paid a hellish price just in surviving this long.

* * * * * * *

For Barry it happened pretty fast. He had known pretty much want to expect when he went to her home. But hadn't expected it to slam into instant action.

Joan was dressed in a bathrobe and it was obvious as hell she was naked under it. The moment the door was closed behind him, she flew into his arms, hands all over him.

When her fingers went directly to *go* and didn't make any effort to be subtle about it, Barry responded, sexually, and fast.

Then her lips were really going to town on him. After getting him hurting-hard, Joan stood, grinning up, said: "I've been needing you, Barry! Oh, how I've been needing you!"

She pulled him to a chair, sitting herself down on it, parting the robe, opening her thighs, and then pulling him between them. It was fast and carnal. The first thrust had obviously hurt Joan a little, because she really wasn't completely ready for him, but she had grabbed his thighs and actually forced his shaft into her, hips jerking real fast and greedy until they both climaxed.

It was obvious that she instinctively knew his need to be sexually taken like a bomb, leaving little room for anything else. A sexual washout to burn away the love-need for Ann.

But it was hardly enough, really. Emotionally he didn't

want sex; yet Joan controlled the raging animal side of him. She was overwhelming.

Later that first night she all but forced him into a shower with her.

The feel of the naked, wet flesh against his body was enough to create quick orgiastic reaction. She'd clutched close. And in the desperate way she took him, standing, Barry wondered about her own frantic need.

Afterwards, she had washed him with her own hands, creating another hard. One part of his mind rebelled against the sex for sex-sake. He kept thinking about Ann; wanting her, desperately. He didn't want anybody other than this woman.

But Joan's own need was frantic; and he knew this woman needed him; and also now realized that she must love him, in her way. But all her kisses, her body, her caresses, just made him remember how much he desired Ann; how much he missed her; how much she meant to him. He submissively allowed himself to be taken by Joan, more for her sake than anything else.

And all the time he couldn't help comparing the two women. Their personalities, bodies, kisses, and love-making. And every time he tried to touch or kiss Joan, that wall of comparison would delay any real passion or great need. It was mere orgasm. An automatic thing, without any emotional feelings.

It wasn't love; it was an orgy of escape; something he realized was meaningless next to sharing love with somebody that counted more than life itself.

Still, what he shared with Joan for so many days made it possible to respond tenderly, at times; for he did care about her—though not with the depth of feeling experienced with Ann.

The first night was merely two bodies lustfully taking, not giving, on his part.

He was actually glad when Joan fell asleep, lying next to him in bed, for it seemed this was a time for waiting. It was the last escape in his life and for that he really had to thank God there was somebody like Joan to help him over this anguished waiting period. It was merely in knowing the difference; in having experienced perfection in Ann's arms, that tormented his total pleasure.

At times he didn't want anything sexual. And she didn't attempt to start anything. Her whole attitude was that of a person waiting, willing and ready to be there when he wanted or needed her.

If it weren't for the way he felt about Ann, he might very well have found a number of reasons to fall in love with Joan in those few days they shared, almost as a married couple. She was wonderful. Kind. Understanding. All that a man might want. The bad seemed to have been left outside, and only the good in her now showed. She wasn't a lush any more. She was a woman who wanted to help in every way she could. A woman in love. And with her man. And content to be there at his side—as if it were forever, rather than a very short time.

In the middle of the first night Joan had awakened, slipped into his arms, clutching close. "Oh, Barry, I just can't get enough of you."

She remained in his arms, almost sobbing, kissing him, and crying with emotion.

And for a moment he had tried to forget about Ann and think only of this woman who was, regardless of all else, a human being alone in the world, hungering for love and affection, somebody to care for her.

Life could be terribly difficult; survival a balancing act that could be crippled by one simple mistaken move. Even under the best of circumstances life was an iffy thing. Those that survived long enough to experience the aging process suddenly face another challenge—and that was the price tag they paid for long survival. For some people death came slamming down in youth or middle age. Nobody knew when it would all end.

And for these moments they were together, as a couple, sharing their mutual space, caring about one another, shutting out the rest of the world, as if it didn't even exist, matter. And in some ways that was all there could ever be.

The moment. The immediate now.

And they were mutually married to that moment during the next days together.

He tried to be only aware of the sensual feel of her body, her lips, her own personal desires as the passion of her body moved erotic actions against him.

Later, she sat up suddenly, left the room, returned with drinks.

Then Joan hit him one below the belt.

"Blacky called me today..." she said, sitting down beside him on the bed. "He wants us to go with Ann and him to Boise, when you fly there to pick Benton and the girls up. He plans a sorta vacation."

He hadn't heard the rest then. All he could think of was the desire to be near Ann. Not to feel her closely held, tightly embraced. Not to kiss her.

Later he learned—he heard the rest.

"Be careful, Barry. He's after something. I don't know what. But you can bet your bottom dollar that he doesn't do anything without a damn good reason. He's a dangerous man."

Had Blacky found out about him and Ann? Guessed? The idea terrified him. Or was it just her imagination? Maybe it *was* only for a few kicks. After all, what were they afraid of? Blacky Jenson was only a man—would, could die like anyone else.

He remembered that nothing had gone on between Ann and himself until *after* the phone call. That saved them there. Or did it?

Yet he realized that this was a time of quiet before the storm. It was only a matter of days, then hell could bloom like an ever expanding whirlpool to suck them into its fiery depths.

They would wait until then. He would have Joan; she would have him.

A determined plan had eaten its way at his mind. Even Joan seemed to be thinking about Saturday, and what might happen to Blacky Jenson when three people who hate his guts would have the man in their power.

Four days of just sitting and waiting. Four days to think of Ann in the arms of Jenson. That bloated thing caressing her delicate body, kissing her.

He didn't think he would make it. Not sober. Not without some means of escape.

Joan seemed to realize how he felt. Seemed to know what misery the days were for him. She was always there, wanting to help him. Out of the pain. Give him the blackout from the ugly reality of each day, hour, minute. Make each moment less bitter.

So they waited together, seeking a way out from their frustrations through the exchange of their bodily passions.

He lost track of time that first evening. Moments faded. Time passed.

The world clouded around him and became a blackish red mist.

In that crimson blindness he heard his voice calling, "Ann—oh, dear God! Ann!" He felt her body, more full than he remembered, more basically animal and demanding—like Joan's. He heard the sobbing cry of a woman's voice repeating his name over and over in desperate pain.

The fog cleared out and he found himself lying in a large chair. Joan was sleeping silently and nakedly on the sofa across from him.

When he stood, a series of jagged spears cut through his brain. The sound of a bottle falling to the floor at his feet was an atomic blast hitting both ear-drums.

Staggering up to the bar he poured himself a water glass full of whiskey.

Joan stirred on the sofa. Her body moved gently; the action had a sexual quality about it. Everything Joan did had a sexual quality about it. Basic and animal. Raw. But in a lovely way.

He gulped at the glass. The liquor touched his stomach with a sting; then everything started numbing. Spinning.

That was good; He didn't want to think. Think about Ann.

Ann. Ann Cummings.

God, how he wanted her.

He took several more swallows of the whiskey and then stepped over to where Joan was sleeping.

The sight of her white skin was a wonderful thing to see. Her form, full and beautiful. Even for a lush she was really some woman. He had to hand her that. His eyes examined

121

every curve and swell. Every inch of her. Every delicious rounded hollow and line.

More liquor smashed into his stomach and blended with his nervous system. And he just stood there looking down at this red-headed beauty—only half conscious that he was doing so. She had a sensual animal look which he examined in minute detail like a scientist might make a study of some new insect or bug they had just discovered.

He didn't know how long he stood watching. He didn't even notice that the glass, now empty, had fallen from his fingers and he was now drinking from the bottle. He swayed a lot. But he remained there, drunkenly fascinated by the flowing grace of her—a womanly form which had been made to respond and excite to a man's will.

Each breath she took caused her body to fall and rise temptingly.

She stirred suddenly. Turned, looked up at him. A slow sensual smile formed on her full lips, and even though there was a hot burn of fire in her eyes, it was mixed with a deep suggestion of pain.

It was funny, Barry thought, *how two people could so easy communicate with their eyes. He could almost read Joan's thoughts, and they were filled with pain.*

He leaned forward, toward her, tenderly kissed her forehead. It was easy to fall into the mood of this woman, of being with her. And most of all it was easy to simply let himself believe any fantasy that fit. She was a wonderful kid. A great lover.

"Hello, beautiful," he murmured against her ear.

"You make me *feel* beautiful, all over, Barry," Joan's lips whispered huskily. "And sexy...but not like when I'm with other men...they are dirty, perverted orgies."

Barry felt a wave of tender emotion for Joan. It was impossible not to care, once you knew her, accept this woman as a human being. Most of all, he understood the pain of loneliness and the hunger for love.

Everybody wanted to be loved, needed, appreciated, and accepted. But most of all, loved.

His hand ran softly across her breasts, aware of the quick hardening of her nipples. He palmed, carefully squeezed one breast while kissing her throat. Then he ran his hand down across her stomach, and into the heat between her thighs. She squirmed up against the touch, trapped his fingers against her warm flesh.

"You feel good, lover!" she breathed.

"You feel good, too, Joan," Barry told her, letting his fingers search tenderly in order to give her a deep sense of loving pleasure.

"Make love to me, please," Joan pleaded in a husky rasp. "Love me very tenderly, as if you mean it."

Those words held a hungry need and were filled with total awareness that he didn't love her. Yet she craved even the illusion that it might be so.

Slowly he withdrew his hand from between her thighs, leaned over, placing a light kiss on each taut nipple, then lovingly ran his kissed all over her body.

She moaned with pleasure. Then he was holding her in his arms, their lips fused, tongues playing in and out.

Somehow she managed to slip her legs over the edge of the sofa, thighs parted, ankles locked about his. Their lips never stopped devouring one another as their hips slipped gently back and forth, up and down. Then abruptly Joan lifted her hips, expertly captured him, and enveloped him deeply within her. They suddenly went wild, immediately moved violently up and down so fast that it was obvious that they were beyond any control, and completely captured in a savage quest for total release. When ecstasy flooded over them, then passed away, he moved, stood, looked down at Joan, who was now leaning back against the sofa, eyes closed, face in contented repose.

He went and fixed himself another drink.

Maybe he had downed two high-balls, he hadn't counted, when Joan's voice called to him.

"Barry...let's have an all-out orgy! No holds barred. Just escape into one another as if our lives depended on it!"

He turned.

She was sitting up on the sofa, looking longingly at him.

"I thought we'd been doing a pretty good job, already," he replied in a flat voice.

"No—I know how things really are, Barry. Between you

and...her! But I don't want to think about it. So—don't mention it!"

Barry interrupted with: "Joan, don't explain."

Her eyes said silently to him that she wanted to help, and most of all, wanted the same kind of total sexual cop-out.

Then suddenly she sprang to her feet, came up to. "Oh, Barry, I feel like...just screaming—every word, every action a...sick-orgy demands."

Her hips surged against his, wiggled. "Once I was a nice girl. Now...now I feel as bitchy as hell! Do you know what I mean?"

The feel of her was exciting.

He reached around and fondled her fanny, smiled, said: "You don't know how much pleasure you would give me!"

They parted, Joan fixed herself a drink and then faced him.

She sipped her drink, said: "There've been so many men who *wanted* filthy sex with me. But I feel different with you, Barry—oh, shit!"

She sighed, then took in a deep breath that expanded her breasts. "Oh, but I'm hungry! For that!"

Her eyes ran down his body, feasting on him.

He laughed, delighted, a sharp excitement striking him as she looked hungrily between his legs. Her words fit the moment; deliciously erotic and pure animal.

"I want you, Barry."

They moved across the room, then finally were standing in front of the bed.

It continued on and off throughout the day and night, exhausting both of them into short sleeps, only to begin once more after rest had soothed their tired bodies.

It was a total orgy.

Never before in his life had he continued on for such a long time, without getting up from bed; with any woman. It was as if this might be his last orgy; an orgy meant to satisfy any man's lifelong desire for such sexual activities.

Somehow, Barry felt that Joan knew their affair was coming to an end and wanted to make the most of what was left.

124

They got up only to refill their drinks.

It was in this way they consumed one another, waiting together for what was so immediate in their future.

Thus they waited together, carnally devouring one another. Waited for Saturday. They lived in a world of passion. They closed it around them and only left her apartment a few times to buy food and booze.

When he had come out of his drunken fog there were only two more days to go. They waited, sometimes making gentle love; sometimes taking one another like savage animals. It was the only way he could momentarily put aside thoughts of Ann, of Blacky Jenson and what was going to happen Saturday.

In those days it was almost as if nothing else existed; as if they were in another world; a fantasy paradise where two lovers took pleasure in endless orgasm. Though even then, there were the quiet moments when she was only lying in his arms; or the conversational moments when they were drinking cocktails or eating. Those were the resting periods; the long pauses between sexual bouts. And because of Joan, because of the woman she was, they became, for the time, the only two real people in the world.

Chapter *FIFTEEN*

Those last days with Barry were a mixture of heaven and hell to Joan. For those days she had him for herself. Completely. Except for the awareness of his emotional attachment to Ann Cummings it might have seemed perfect. It wasn't mentioned much, but it was always there, between them. A cutting knife that reminded her how little she was getting, how little she could grab for herself; how little life had to offer, or ever would offer. At the most, these were the happiest moments she would ever experience.

Yet she was able at times, long and delightful moments, to forget, to imagine that they were lovers on their honeymoon together. Lovers for eternity. It was a fantasy, but a beautiful one for her.

Joan, the girl who had once held romantic dreams. Joan Verril, glamorous movie star, who ended up photographing models, starlets, show girls, call girls, whores, sluts, anything in panties that would come and pose for her half naked, or fully stripped.

Not all the girls had been easy marks for the producers, directors and the rest of the Hollywood casting-couchers, but there had been one hell of a lot.

Joan Verril became a lush and easy make for the first man willing to caress her body, soothing the ache which Blacky Jenson had brought out in her. Blacky Jenson; small time hood, who dealt in human lives; dope rings, smuggling, call girls, bookies, dirty political machines.

She almost hated Jenson more than she loved Barry. She *did* hate him more than she loved life.

Yet she couldn't forget that it was Blacky who had brought her Barry. The one nice thing he had done for her—without any knowledge of what he'd really given her. But

126

too late. It was too late to grab Barry for herself. Too late to keep him forever. Maybe a year ago he might have given her a serious tumble. But now. No. Way.

No man wanted a lush. And she couldn't change. Even for Barry. For she couldn't stop drinking and wanting men—ever, as long as she lived. She was as helpless in her need as a dope addict—as badly ruined.

Her life after Barry had gone would be worse than before. For now she would have memory of something better, which could never be hers, never be attained again.

For that, she hated Blacky, Barry and Ann Cummings.

She hated Ann with a difference. She couldn't blame the girl. It wasn't her fault. Barry was emotionally drawn to Ann before he had ever met Joan.

And she realized to him, she was the same as she was to any other man—a good lay.

That was it. The finish. The complete beginning and end. Always that little monster that pulled her into nothing; that left her helpless with her own desires and passions; sexual lusts, that left nothing else for her except escape, and drinking.

No. No man would want a woman like her. It was too late for her.

But not too late for Ann. Not too late for Barry and Ann. They had a chance. They had the opportunity to escape together and help each other and be with each other. They could find escape, and meaning for life. If but given a way. If only allowed. But Blacky Jenson wasn't about to give them that chance.

And Joan knew it. She also knew that maybe somebody else might step in and see to it that they *did* get that chance.

Maybe during the trip up to Boise, Blacky Jenson would suddenly disappear; fall out of the plane.

She liked the thought. She went warm inside. Cold. Then warm.

That was a way out. An out for everybody. A way to make meaning to her own life. A way to escape for all of them. Get rid of Jenson, and all their problems would be over. Kill Blacky, and the world would be just that much better off. Nobody decent would miss him, and those who did really didn't count.

It was an idea. A good one.

That would give meaning—some reason for her having gone through such hell. Some payment back to Blacky for what he had done to her, to Ann and all the other girls before, and all those who might follow.

Those were the planning moments. The moments away from Barry's arms. The times she began thinking. Thinking, And thinking.

Thankfully, they weren't many.

She couldn't think straight while near Barry; not while being kissed, held, caressed and made love to—even drunken love. During the last days she had become wildly orgiastic, both in her words and actions.

There were times of crazed passion, times of loving gentle union.

All blended together in her mind; all became a beautiful, endless orgy of love. Even when she wasn't in his arms she experienced a thrilling sense of pleasure far deeper than other men could give even at the moment of an orgiastic climax.

And because of that, Joan couldn't keep her hands off him, even in quiet moments of sitting or lying close together. Her fingers always found him.

The time with Barry wasn't so much continual lovemaking, without breaks; for there were many long hours when they did and said nothing; or slept together; or drank and ate. What conversation they exchanged was more in glances than words. What words were actually spoken were meaningless and easily forgotten almost while mouthed.

In his arms or merely near him, Joan discovered that her thoughts were always full of emotional feelings of love. Even when Barry was too drunk to perform or to be anything other than a beast and animal with her body, using it like most men always had, her love for him was one of the strongest emotions she really felt. And because of, or despite, this, she found some form of strange contentment. A haunting happiness; no matter what, she possessed a man who needed her almost as much as she needed him—even if the reasons were different. For the moment she was totally

128

his; he was totally hers to have and hold and love.

Thus, she lived out a mental fantasy, trying to believe it would never end; escaping into the dream-like make-believe that this wonderful man would never leave. And because he was always there after having carnally or lovingly possessed her body, it was an easy dream to believe—for the moment.

They were oddly happy days. Happy with this man she so desperately loved.

She took what she could get. Forgot the future. Embraced and received what was openly offered. Much like she had always done; except this time it was for the love.

Then suddenly it was over. Too soon the day came when her life slashed back to reality and she became the slutting lush men used and left behind.

Saturday!

Chapter *SIXTEEN*

It was a bad day for flying. In both ways. The sky was cloudy and overcast, a storm was threatening to hit the west coast, and heavy winds were already beginning to build. Then there was the inner emotional storm which he faced, and that terrified him most of all.

He had seen Ann briefly, one arm locked in Blacky Jenson's. Smiling, but impersonal acting toward Barry.

That had been the hard part.

Appearing to hardly know each other. Making believe, when his insides worked in him like he had just taken a large swallow of poisonous acid.

Jenson was smiling. Laughing. Joking. But deadly serious—as usual. "Okay, flyboy, let's get the show rolling, I can't wait all day long. *We* have a party waiting for us in Boise, a real live party—some of the boys who want to show little old Blacky the ropes in their fair city. So, let's fly away into the sky."

The man's hand slapped down on Barry's shoulder, rubbing it in a friendly gesture. He didn't like being pawed by another man. He didn't know how much of this man he would be able to stand, before the welling hate took control of his will. How much of being so near Ann and doing nothing about it, saying nothing to her.

Joan seemed to be withdrawn, not showing any emotion. He felt sorry for her. He knew how she felt toward him. He knew and wished there was something he could do about it. But there wasn't anything anyone could do. Not a thing.

He refueled Nelly, checked over the controls, and then started the engine as Joan sat silently next to him in the co-pilot's seat. He directed the plane down to the landing strip, and seconds later was slowly letting Nelly free to lift up off

130

the ground and into the air.

They were on their way. Their long way. A trip that was supposed to end at Boise—and would end somewhere short of that destination.

There were too many emotions pent up in this little tin-can. Too many hates, directed toward the same man. All three of them wanted Jenson out of the way. Yet none of them were killers. None had killed before.

Barry turned to Joan.

"Well?" he smiled, patting her leg affectionately. He felt close to her, in a more brotherly fashion now. If one could think of a woman whose body had been such a sensual pleasure as a sister.

No, the emotion really was something different. Something deeper.

Maybe if it hadn't been for Ann, he might have found himself falling in love with her. He knew he didn't believe it. Not really. But it had been a good thought. A good idea. He wished with all his mind that it were so—for Joan's sake. With everything in him. She had revealed an inner quality, the last couple of days, of selflessness which he hadn't realized she possessed. It had shown a small spark of what she might have been if people like Jenson had left her alone.

"Here we are..." she smiled back. It was mechanical, without emotion. A muscular movement. Joan seemed to be gone now. The Joan he had known that last couple of days. The heart was finished. Only a dead being living in a robotic shell was left.

"Buck up, Joanie, it isn't the end of the world!" he said, trying to sound cheerful. But he didn't feel happy. He felt like hell. He felt as if he were betraying his best friend.

That was it. He had never felt closer to anybody before, without being in love with them in some way. There were, no doubt about it, different kinds of love. And what he felt for Joan was a form of love, a caring, a bond that would remain forever as a special reality all its own.

That thought stopped him.

It was foolish for anyone to think that they had only room enough in their emotions to love but one person. Of course he loved Joan—but in that different way. "You know,

Joan...I don't know quite how to tell you. Well, you've been a real sport. I mean—"

"I know..." she smiled. This time she was alive. Just for a sparking instant. "But...don't say anything you don't mean."

"It's not that...I've just never known anyone like you. These last two days...well, I wouldn't have been able to make it. Not at all!"

He reached over and pulled her closer to him. Kissing her lightly on the lips, he whispered: "If things had been different...I..."

She stiffened. "Don't—*please!* Don't say it! It would hurt too much...too unfair!"

They were silent. They moved apart. It was now over with them. Completed. Finished. And they both knew it. The affair; the emotions; the actions; the fantasy of love—that really was only a desperate need to escape from the reality which had been around them.

This last moment had been it. Now it was business. A business of going through with something that neither had any guts to do. But must do. They hadn't spoken about it. They hadn't even given much conscious thought to it. Yet, there it was.

They were alone with Blacky Jenson. Two women and a man. All three hated the fat guy's guts. It wouldn't be easy— yet, not too hard either.

The two of them knew that Ann was aware of the feeling, the realization. It would be simple.

If someone would just kill Jenson. Open a door and drop him out.

It would be a *snap,* Barry realized, *so very simple.*

He stood and opened the door which led to the passenger compartment. "All out for Boise," he laughed cheerfully.

"So *soon?*" Ann asked. Her voice had the edge of alarm and terror. For a moment Barry thought she must have really believed him: *or thought he was about to give Jenson the push!*

He tried to laugh. But didn't quite make it.

Blacky was in the back of the long compartment, at a small nook in the corner, looking through some papers he had brought in his briefcase. He hardly noticed that Barry and Joan had joined them.

Barry looked at Ann and saw the fear in her eyes. Her lips were white rimmed and trembling.

It's funny, he thought, forcing himself to look away, *how people could communicate so completely with their eyes...No word spoken...Just a sudden exchange of emotional ideas...ideas as complete and complicated as the agreed upon murder of another human being. Not a word...Yet they all knew what must be done! This was an ideal chance which might never re-create itself.*

"This is sure a cheerful group of ghouls!" Joan's voice laughed from behind him.

He shook himself. *This was ridiculous! Completely fantastic! Here he was, thinking and planning murder, and convincing himself that Ann and Joan were thinking and planning it too. It was completely fantastic!*

But true.

He couldn't deny that. He couldn't shake that thought out of his mind. All he needed to do, to convince himself of its truth, was to look into either of the girls' eyes. They told the same information. Showed the same emotions. The same hates. The same desires. The same plan.

Kill Jenson while we have the chance! Rid the world of a real no good bastard!

Another shudder moved through him, because he knew that somehow, sometime, somewhere between Los Angeles and Boise, Blacky Jenson, small time hood, smuggler, bookie, call girl racketeer, and other allied crimes, no doubt including murder, would suddenly stop living.

Who would it be? Who would be the one?

His muscles went tense and his guts hurt worse than they ever had. It *should* be himself. He wondered if he would be able to kill the man.

He looked at Blacky Jenson and the hates returned, and the determination—and he saw a dead man!

Two hours had passed since the four of them had taken off from Los Angeles. Two hours. And half the flight almost over. And nothing had been done. Yet.

* * * * * * *

Joan felt ill. Maybe it was the flying. They had been through some rough weather. Even if Barry did claim that air sickness was all in the head. Maybe it was her nerves.

Maybe the lack of liquor.

That was funny. For months she had been thinking of nothing but drinks and getting a man for the night. Now her whole life was changed. Her emotions keyed up and involved with different things, and motives; and ideas; passions.

Now it was murder. All else seemed to lack reality. Jenson had to be done away with. Like you would kill a deadly bug, or insect that is harming a beautiful flower bed. Like a gangrenous arm that would have to be cut off to save the man. He was a disease, like all of his kind. People should go out of their way to squash such things, like they would do away with a cockroach. It wasn't as if they planned to kill a human being. He wasn't human. he didn't deserve the title.

At least she didn't think he did.

Maybe she was wrong. What right did anyone like herself have to condemn anyone else? A lush, a tramp. A good lay for any man who wanted to take her

As low as she was—maybe that gave her *more* of a right.

She was a disease too. She was the weakness that plagued mankind. And because of that she was in the same gutter as Jenson and men like him. Because of the wreckage she had made of her life, she was able to see the real meanness in others who wallowed in the same gutter. This man enjoyed the power he used over others around him; people weren't living beings, merely things to be used, abused and then kicked out, aside, to give to the begging dogs.

Her mouth felt dry. Her stomach nervous. It jumped at every movement that anyone made.

Nobody had said anything for what seemed hours. All seemed to be waiting to see what the other would do.

Blacky Jenson just sat in his corner, studying papers. Saying nothing. Unaware that anybody was with him.

Two hours and nothing happened.

134

Maybe she should be the one. It would be best.

JOAN VERRIL KILLS BLACKY JENSON!

She could see it in the headlines. That would look good.
"What time is it?" she asked Barry.

He jumped, as if shot. Looked at his watch and said: "Five forty-five..." His voice was dead. A flat statement. No emotion.

They seemed to be waiting for the fairy-goddess to come down and wave her magic wand that would eliminate their problem for them.

They were a nice bunch of cowards. A pilot who didn't mind getting involved in shady deals. A woman who liked to drink too much and make men too much. Another woman who was the mistress of a gangster.

A real nice trio.

Plotting. Silently plotting murder.

And that was the veal joke! Not one of them had spoken a word about their thoughts, desires, or plans. They all knew what the other two were thinking, as if they were attached to one central mind.

And in a way that was true.

They all had the same single boring bell ringing in their brains. A bell that didn't say dingdong, but said: Kill-kill, kill-kill.

Over and over.

She stood and started walking to where Blacky Jenson sat. *Now was as good a time to do it as any.*

But what with? That thought stopped her.

She looked desperately at Barry who was half in the air, suspended above his seat, ready to move forward, ready to stop her. His hands were already reaching out in her direction.

She shrugged and sat down. *How?*

How...?

* * * * * * *

They were coming in toward the airport. Barry's stomach was knotted upon itself with disgust.

Nobody had done anything. They had just sat around and waited.

Several times he had started. But then one excuse after another stopped him. First it was the cold sweat that had worked over his body. Then it was the shaky feeling of his muscles.

Wait just a little while longer. Then—then, maybe!

But minutes had dragged longer and longer, until hours had passed. Joan had stopped twice. The first time stopping herself. The second time he had stopped her.

It wasn't up to a woman.

He should do it.

But always there had been a good reason for waiting. How was he to do it? Or should he give the man a chance? That ol' shootout at the OK corral.

Ann had gotten up once, her face white and drawn. But she'd only taken two steps and then sat down again, trembling.

Then they had waited. Glancing at one another. Seeing the guilt. The fear. The defeat. The hungry, desperate animal desire to kill; naked and outright. But mostly they hadn't looked at anything but their own hands or the floor. No meeting of eyes had been longer than fast, fleeting contacts, that sought escape from the knowledge of what all of them planned, and waited for; and were afraid to do!

Savagely he worked the controls in his hands. Gripping hard, until his knuckles were bloodless. Sweat was drenching his clothing. Twice he had circled the landing field, making false attempts, and then zooming upwards again.

Stalling.

Hoping for some miracle to happen. Something to take the life of Blacky Jenson. Then it happened. Too fast for him to stop. Too quick to do anything about. First the cockpit door opened. The thick, heavy features of Blacky poked in.

"What the hell's going on?" he bellowed in a heated, tight lipped voice. "Can't you land this damn thing?"

Then a thin, strained, high pitched hysterical voice cried from the passenger compartment behind him, "Why doesn't someone kill him now?—*now!*"

136

Chapter *SEVENTEEN*

When Ann had gotten up, Joan's heart stopped. It started again when she sat down again.

The girl wouldn't have done it anyway, she thought, *she hasn't gone that far...yet; it's between Barry and myself.*

Then she started to get up, and felt Barry's hand stop her.

Okay—you do it, then! But nothing had happened. Minutes dragged. Then an hour. And another.

Barry got up for the last time and went into the cockpit and took over the controls from the automatic pilot. Every time before when he'd checked the flight course there had been an expression of eager excitement and even once in awhile relief, but this time it was only a look of total defeat.

It was over. Finished. Too late. Nobody had done anything. Not a thing. They had all chickened out.

Maybe that was why they were failures in life. Why they had ended up under the thumb of this Blacky Jenson man. If not him, some other SOB would have been their master. Maybe that was why that kind of man got into power in the first place, and stayed there. Because nobody had any guts.

They had failed in life. They had allowed themselves to be ground under, ruined by a meaner, more powerful man whom they couldn't kill even when given the chance.

It was a laugh. Jenson would never know how close he had come to dying. He would never know that he had just missed it by inches.

Or had he?

Maybe he had known. Maybe he had been aware of their hate, and had put them all here alone with him. Together to silently plot...plan.

And do nothing!

137

To fail, face the reality that they were living pawns to be played with by a chess master like himself.

Maybe he realized that they would never be able to kill him, or anybody else, because they were so weak.

Maybe he was giving a little demonstration of his total power over them, so that he could grind them down some more.

She didn't like that thought. Not at all. She preferred to think that he had never known, that in his self-conceit could never admit that anyone would dare hate him or dislike him. *But how childish of her.*

No one could be that dumb. He must know that some hated—yet how could he guess about the three of them? One was his loving mistress, another an ex-mistress whom he knew to be a lush, and weak, helpless. He might suspect her of hate, but not of having the courage to kill. But Barry had no reason to feel anything toward Blacky—not as long as you didn't know about his feeling toward Ann.

And Blacky couldn't know anything about that, unless one of the three had told him; and none of them had. None had any motive except herself—*and she hadn't!*

So close; too close. And nobody had done anything about it.

It was a long time since Barry had gone into the cockpit. They seemed to have been circling for a long, terribly long period of time.

She wondered what had gone wrong Then Blacky looked up in their direction. His face was puzzled-looking.

"I thought we were landing..." he grumbled, starting to stand. "What the hell's wrong with that flyboy? Can't he land a plane?"

"Oh, he'll..." Ann started to explain, then stopped as Blacky moved toward them. Her voice seemed to freeze in mid-air. Her expression flushed into one of almost terror.

Joan felt herself go tense. Hot and cold. Fear and thrill.

After he passed them, he poked his head into the cockpit, cursing: *"What the hell's going on? Can't you land this damn thing?"*

Ann screamed, clutching her hand in frantic frustration: "Why doesn't somebody kill him now?—*now!*"

138

Joan leaped to her feet as Blacky turned, an ugly expression on his face. He looked for a long moment at Ann. It seemed like the world frosted over as his eyes became darker and his expression grimmer with fury.

"What's that you said? What's that you said?" he yelled, stepping forward and swinging a beefy open hand across her face.

The impact of that blow threw the girl back in her seat, hard and violently.

"What you say?" Jenson screamed in a loud choking voice, moving closer and slapping her again and again. "You little, damn bitch! You cheap little whore!"

Joan was horrified. She couldn't move. What was going on made her spin with rage and disgust; it paralyzed her with hatred.

Then Barry leaped out from the cockpit, jumped at Jenson and twisted the man around to meet the impact of a fast flying, murderous fist. It connected at the throat. Barry's face was flushed red. He stood half sobbing with uncontrolled fury and madness, as he pounded Jenson's body and face with one savage blow after another. The other man was too stunned, physically shocked and hurt to do anything but whimper and scream his agony. Blood spurted from his broken nose, his lips became torn and red smeared.

Then everything seemed to slide upside down and for a moment she didn't remember anything but sickness. Everything spun and she found herself doubled over, violently ill, her stomach muscles convulsively jerking. She was aware that Ann, Barry and Jenson were tangling and twisting all around her.

The plane was spinning, diving toward the ground, out of control.

* * * * * * *

Barry had heard the scream. The sound of struggle. Jenson's voice, and then what could be nothing except one person hitting another. He didn't have to guess what had happened—he knew!

Without any thought he leaped from his seat. A purple

cloud was drowning his vision. He simply jumped toward the door, flinging himself at Jenson. He wasn't even thinking about what he was doing. The volcano had exploded into reality and he was smashing it out at the one person who was responsible.

His mind was racing. His body and fists and lungs and every nerve and muscle responding to the hate which had been in him for so many days now.

Jenson! The dirty bastard who dared to hit women! Who dared to have even touched Ann!

The world began to spin around him and he automatically became aware of what had happened. The years of training pushed aside the rage and brought half-sanity to his mind.

The plane was diving! The controls were going wild! He had left them to their own devices. He had to get to the controls!

His vision and awareness cleared. At the same time he saw that Blacky Jenson's throat was in his hands. The face that looked up at him was a horrid purple distortion of what he had once known to be such a hard, cold, powerful little man. The expression was filled with pain and terror; fear. No glory showed. Only agony.

Blood was smeared all over the features. Red and pulpy where the nose had been almost torn off. The lips and jaw were flowing with red foam. The man's tongue was puffy and swollen.

Barry realized that he was looking into the face of a slowly choking man. He was killing him with his bare hands.

That shocked him to complete sanity.

Then he remembered the spinning, downward fall of the plane.

The plane.

The controls! his mind screamed, frantically.

He had to finish killing Blacky!

They were diving to their deaths.

It didn't matter, any more. They'd all be dead.

Quickly he untangled himself from Jenson and worked his way into the pilot's seat. Desperately he fought with the controls, bringing the plane into a parallel with the ground. It

140

took a lot of effort and a lot of strength and a lot of time. Time enough to realize what had just taken place a moment before.

He'd almost killed a man!

The thought sickened him. It sobered his mind. No matter how bad Blacky Jenson was, the man wasn't worth dying for; he wasn't worth going to jail for. And killing the man wouldn't really solve any of Barry's problems; only make them worse.

But what could they do about the man. What would Blacky want to do to them—if he lived?

Yet how would it be possible to simply cold-bloodedly kill even a monster like this man?

Never had he been so close to killing a person in his life. Never again did he want to come that close.

After setting the plane on automatic pilot, he stood and started to turn.

A strangled voice which he hardly recognized as Jenson's came to his ears. *"I'll kill him...I'll kill all of you!"*

He knew then that the fight wasn't really over after all. The rage was gone, but the battle still had to be fought.

He rushed forward and then came to a dead stop. A shocked dead stop.

"Stay right where you are, everybody!" Joan's voice said, coldly. In her hands was a small, ugly .38 revolver.

* * * * * * *

First, there had been the spinning and the sickness and then, after what seemed an eternity, the plane up righted and Joan found herself in a tangle with Jenson. Her reaction was horror. Then her eyes saw something black, shiny and ugly in a leather holster under his jacket. A gun.

He was moaning and in pain, but conscious and gaining strength by the minute. "I'll kill him..." the gangster cried in a strangled voice, starting to reach for his weapon. "I'll kill all of you!"

Frantically she groped for the gun. Jenson was physically weakened and dazed by the beating Barry had given him; it wouldn't be hard to overpower him—*to kill him!*

That was impossible!

But.

She had to stop him in any case. There was no telling what the man might or would do. If he said he'd kill, chances were he'd do just that; regardless of the fact that Barry was the only person there who could land the plane safely.

Blacky Jenson was somewhat crazed under normal circumstances; now the man was quite mad in his fury. He would simply act. Murderously.

Then suddenly the gun was in her fingers. She gripped it hard, while at the same time kicking the still dazed man away, with her foot. He slid backwards several feet, shock and surprise showing in his face.

"Stay right where you are. Everybody!" she ordered, threatening Jenson with the gun. "Don't move! You either, Barry!"

She couldn't use the gun on Barry, but he wouldn't be quite sure of that, at first. It would stop him long enough; just long enough for her to do what she had to. What she had to do to give reason and meaning to her life. Give a meaning which she had never been able to get before this very moment.

She was afraid, even terrified. Sweating. But sure of what she would do. It would take only one split second. Only an instant.

"Don't do it, Joan," Barry's voice shouted, pleadingly. "It's not worth it! He's not worth it!"

She didn't care any more. It was cold blooded murder, but she couldn't care less. She just aimed and fired.

It surprised her how simple it was. To kill a big man or a small man it was all the same; all you did was point a gun in his direction and pull the trigger. Just squeeze your finger.

No! One didn't even pull the trigger. Just the act of aiming and desiring—her whole body had simply clamped around the moment, and the gun was alive.

It all happened in one swift instant; one decisive act.

No words. No pleading for life. No court of law. No police. No legal mess or complications. No threats. Nothing.

He didn't look so important dying. His expression of shock and hurt didn't look so powerful. So threatening.

142

Just a fat man who was slowly dying.

"You...You!" he moaned, clutching his stomach, the blood with seeping out between his fingers. "God! Oh, hell!"

Surprise was blanching his face white and horrible. "You bitch, You've...you...killed me!" Then he started to rise threateningly toward her. Reaching out. Attempting to get at the person who had done this horrible, unjust thing to him.

She pulled the trigger again. But it was a frantic action. Nothing happened. Either there wasn't a bullet in the chamber or it was merely a dud. Then he was upon her. She struggled, thinking at first she would be able to push him easily off. But that was a mistake; a deadly one.

He was stronger. Even in his dying moments. Every muscle seemed to be bent on taking the gun from her. He was twisting her wrist. It hurt, painfully. His body was pressing her backwards with its heavy weight. She pulled on the trigger in desperation, knowing she had to kill him *now,* before it was too late.

The sound of the gun going off was deadened by the searing burn that erupted in her chest.

* * * * * * *

The explosion of the second bullet shattered the air. Barry couldn't believe his eyes. Up to that point neither Ann nor he had moved; they were both shocked. Things had happened too fast.

There was a long silence after that. Jenson was now relaxed in death. But Joan's expression revealed where the second bullet had gone. First surprise and then a slight smile passed across her face. She looked at Barry for a long time and then coughed. A red trickle moved from her lips and then her head dropped.

He heard Ann scream.

A hard knot was in Barry's throat as he moved to where Joan lay, very quiet and still. He bent down and looked tenderly at her.

One glance was all that he needed.

They were both dead. Quite still and dead.

He felt his insides turn to acid and then start pushing up

through his throat. His eyes misted, emotionally. Then he was sick. Horribly, violently, and terribly sick.

Barry's first reaction, after he had recovered from the mental shock of what had just taken place, was to head for Mexico. Not land. Just keep on going and never look back.

Then he realized that there was nothing to do but turn themselves in. Tell their story, and hope to God that someone believed them. Chances were pretty good that they'd get off Scot free, or at most with a light sentence, because with the information the two of them possessed, they would help break open the entire racket; maybe even reach the big boys upstairs that Denny Benton had told him about.

Anyway it was the only thing they could do. They couldn't run. To run would mean they'd have to continue to do so all the rest of their lives.

From both the law and the people connected with Jenson. Their only hope was that they let the law deal out the justice where it should morally fall.

No words needed to be exchanged between the two of them. Ann expressed full understanding in her eyes when they looked up into his.

They couldn't run. If they faced what was ahead, honestly, without trying to make excuses, they had a pretty good chance to get out of it and find final freedom together.

They both walked to the cockpit. He took over the controls. He looked at Ann, as she sat next to him in the co-pilot's seat.

It wouldn't be long before they were free; he felt sure of that. They both knew it. The money Jenson had paid him he could turn over to the authorities—or use it to pay for legal advice. When the time came, he would know what was best and right to do. All he knew was that he didn't want to have any part of the dirty money.

He had what he wanted. Ann. He smiled across at her, and she smiled back, almost happily.

It was the first time he had really seen her so completely happy. They had gone through a lot together that afternoon, but they also had gained a lot. They had each other.

Neither was thinking of Joan, who had failed so terribly in life—but made such a dramatic, almost heroic exit. They

144

were only thinking about themselves now. They had earned that right—the hard way.

They would be together, facing all and every problem the world might have to offer them; unafraid and willing to give it a good fight, even if they lost in the end.

In a few minutes they would be facing the most difficult challenge in their lives—but he knew they would win.

"We'll make it okay," he said, squeezing her hand.

She nodded. Leaned over and kissed his cheek.

"I know it, darling. I know."

But they faced a very uncertain future that could easily close in around them like a horrid cruel monster.

Chapter *EIGHTEEN*

The moment they landed things started to move fast. It was out of their hands. They just reacted. And he realized that they had never had any choice about it. The trap had been set already. Jenson's career had drawn to a close a long time before that afternoon. The law had already started reaching out to claw down the world that Blacky had built around himself, even before his sudden, unexpected death.

No sooner had they brought the plane to a stop and started to step out onto the landing field at Boise, than they heard the sound of a siren fill the air. They touched ground and the police car came up opposite them. Several men got out, two in uniform and the other in street clothes.

"Okay, just stay where you are!" one called out at them. "Don't make a move."

They hadn't planned to.

They froze.

Barry couldn't, at first, figure the whole thing out. It was happening too fast. Then he remembered what Hawk-face Denny Benton had told him some days before. The man had warned him that the law might he closing in any moment; that the syndicate boys were about to put an end to Jensen's business operation and turn them over to another, more easily controlled man.

One trip to the D.A.'s office and the career of Blacky Jenson was finished for good.

That probably explained it. But he was too dazed to really think about anything logically. The human mind could only accept so much information at one time and it would numb up, guarding itself of any more shocks.

Anyway, it didn't make any difference as far as Ann and he were concerned. Their fate was already starting to close in on them. They had made their decision and were willing to follow through with it. If this did anything, it just made things easier, Instead of having to go to the police, the police had come to them.

"Where's Jenson?" one man asked, moving up to them.

"In there," Barry motioned behind him, at the plane. "Okay, Jenson, come on out. Do it peacefully and nobody gets hurt."

"Don't bother. He can't hear you. Just go on in, you'll find him," Barry told the man.

The officer stepped slowly closer. He wasn't taking any chances.

Several other cars pulled up and suddenly Barry and Ann found themselves surrounded by a crowd of police and newspaper men. Flashbulbs blinded them on every turn. A couple of plainclothesmen stepped up, one on each side.

"Jensen's dead!" a voice shouted from the plane. "There's a woman in here with him. She's dead too."

"Okay, buster," a voice rasped at his ear, "Want to explain?"

"Simple enough," Barry remarked, trying to sound as casual as possible. After all, he was just telling the truth, there was no reason to be nervous. But that was exactly what he was: scared to death. It was one thing to face a possible jail sentence, and quite another to be going through *it*. He felt almost sick at the stomach. Little insects were crawling along the inside of his guts. If it hadn't been for the tight clutching of Ann's hand *in* his, he didn't know what he might have done. "They killed each other."

"Sure...sure. Likely story!

"Okay," another voice said, "Come along with us."

For some reason the voices seemed to be coming from the air around them; they had no physical identities. They had no bodies of their own. He saw the people, but the forms were just shadows before his eyes. The Voices were the only conscious awareness he had of what or who was speaking to him.

He realized that his mind had gone into a protective daze. It responded only to the things which were important for its survival; nothing more. Voices gave commands; they questioned—they directed, He didn't have to see *who* was speaking to him: that wasn't necessary. Just *what* they said counted.

Just respond with truth, his mind kept saying, *and nothing of real harm could come to you.*

Or Ann.

Ann!

He was worried about her.

Looking at her delicate form as they moved forward, it gave him a pang of regret. Maybe they should have tried to make it to Mexico.

No!

That wouldn't have brought them happiness. It would not have done but ruin any relationship they might have in the future.

They had to face what was ahead; face the results of their past actions and then, maybe, if they were lucky, enjoy a life together that was free from fear and free from any possible legal action that might catch up with them. If they could see this through, together, they would finally have each other and a future of happiness. But before the happiness came there would have to be hell

This was hell! And he had to go through with it. Face the truth and any possible consequence which might follow. That was what had to be done; because he was tired of running and always trying to escape. That had been his trouble all his life. Trying to escape.

During the war was the only time he had ever really faced up to reality; but that had been different—there had been no choice.

Yet, there wasn't any choice now, either.

Ann smiled. Her lips were white-rimmed, but her eyes seemed almost calm. She was scared, he could tell that, just like he was; but she wasn't about to lose control of her emotions or nerve. She wasn't about to give up; or break down. In that way they were much alike; once their minds were made up, they kept to their decision. It was making them up that had been hard.

Ann was really some woman!

"This is a hell of a way to celebrate a new relationship,"

he remarked, attempting to smile and sound light-hearted. The words seemed empty of any emotion. It didn't do any good, he realized. The facts were quite simple. They were about to face the most difficult trial in their lives: an emotional test of their mental makeup. They were about to be forced to live through hell.

They were directed into the back seat of a squad car. The door closed as a policeman sat next to them. "You're in plenty of trouble, mister. I hope, for your sake, you have some answers."

"We do."

The car started off.

It didn't seem fair. But life never was fair. Things never really worked out the way they were supposed to. You planned, struggled and attempted to make a little happiness for yourself. *And what happened?*

But then, if he was honest with himself, he had to admit they were getting exactly what they deserved. Both of them were far from innocent. They weren't free of sin, in this case, They had each gotten involved in a dirty racket, surrounded with dirty little men and all for just a little personal gain. Money or position. They had chosen the way out. Knowing where it might end. Well it was ending where it would, and always had ended: in the gutter!

Still, what else had he expected would happen?

"Hey, buddy, we're here."

He looked at the policeman who was opening the door for them. The man helped Ann out and then motioned him to follow.

Boise, Idaho. Small town; capital of a state. Nothing much more could be said about the place. Except it was where they must finally face themselves and their lives and be willing to accept the results.

As he stepped out of the car, his eyes made contact with Ann's. She was standing on the sidewalk, silently watching him, the policeman next to her.

A shiver ran through her delicate frame. Her eyes seemed to hold an inner hopelessness. Fear. Questions. Concern.

"Don't worry, things will work out," he told Ann, placing an arm around her. He didn't really believe his own words. But he had to say something that might help her to get through this ordeal.

Actually she was basically free of any real crime. Once it was established that Jenson and Joan had killed each other. She'd only been Jensen's mistress. As far as the law was concerned it wouldn't be too hard to prove that she didn't know much about his dealings and business affairs.

"We'll knock them dead!" he whispered, trying to sound unconcerned.

"Sure...sure." Her voice held no conviction.

* * * * * * *

The next few hours whipped by so fast that he didn't even have a chance to think things out. First there was the statement to make. He told the basic facts of what had taken place in the plane. Ann apparently did the same thing. They were questioned separately, but from what the Captain said, their stories checked each other out—which was, actually, all that they *could* do. The truth was the truth. There wasn't anything to add to that.

Then he was booked! On suspicion of murder and the Mann Act charges. A few minutes later he found himself in a cell with his old friend, Denny Benton.

Just the guy he wanted to spend the rest of his days with! "151 Rummy Denny!"

The moment the door opened, Benton stepped up, smiling and looking almost happy to see him. "I didn't think you'd remember *that* bit!"

"How could I help it? My head the next morning. How could I ever forget?" The conversation was ridiculous. Pointless noise.

The man reached out his arm and patted Barry on the back. "I see they hauled you in, too."

"Guess so.

He felt like talking to anybody—especially Benton — like he felt like having a hole put in his head. All he wanted to do was drop into a dead sleep. Sleep out the waiting period. Put himself into a state of suspended animation. Live in a half world until the whole thing was finished and done with. But now he didn't know exactly what was going to happen. How things might work out.

Surely, it seemed to him, it would be easy enough to prove they didn't have anything to do with the murder of Jenson and Joan. The finger prints on the gun would show that. The short range of the shooting should be easily established.

But...what about the other things?

The call-girl racket.

That was one thing that could really turn out to be serious.

Everything else that had happened to him could be written off as just on the edge of the law, but not something that he could be prosecuted for. Still, once a person was sucked into the legal system they were sunk! People's careers could zoom upwards on the right conviction. And DA's didn't give a damn about justice, only in padding their conviction sheet. They took the attitude that if you weren't guilty of this crime, chances were you were guilty of something, maybe even more terrible! *We got ya, baby!* So, it didn't look good. Nothing looked good in the least. And all he wanted to do was escape.

Have a drink.

Do anything in order to not have to think about the jam he had gotten himself into.

And now, for the first time, he began wondering just how he *had* gotten involved in such a life or why. When he had been much younger, he would never have thought of doing some of the things he had done. Not that he had ever been connected with anything that might hurt others; that had been one of his codes of life—to keep from trying to cause harm to others in any direct way. His job for Jenson had been bluntly put:

Illegal!

Face it! No matter how thin he spread the facts, they still spelled out the same thing: he had allowed himself to find time easy way out.

Maybe it was just a matter of getting all wound up and not knowing a way out. You got into the trap of life and somehow didn't realize exactly how bad things had gotten; or how involved.

He had drifted. With no plan of action. Just drifted through life, taking the easy path; not attempting to solve problems, but instead, trying to side-step them or move around them; or find the easy solution.

Life became a sink, which drained you down its tubes and into the gutter, if you let it do that. And he had willingly embraced the easy solution. The pathway of least resistance.

Now, for the first time, for a long time, he was forced to face the results of his actions; and he didn't *like* where it might land him. In Jail. For years, possibly. And that thought terrified him.

It didn't seem right. One mistake could ruin his life forever. He had just found meaning and reason for life with Ann, and to have his freedom snatched away, now, didn't seem fair.

Yet, in the legal sense, that was exactly what could happen.

Still, there might be some chance that he would get out of the jam; maybe a light sentence. The one which he had tried to believe in when he was up in the plane with Ann and the dead bodies of Joan arid Jenson.

His head was hurting from thinking too hard!

He needed a drink. But there wasn't any. And there wouldn't be any for him, for a long time; *if ever.*

He had to do something to keep from thinking. But there wasn't any way of escaping that tick-tick-ticking of his brain. he had to face the facts; and wait out the time; and stay here, in this cell with Hawky; and talk, maybe. Be pleasant.

"Don't you feel like yakking it up?"

The question came out of nowhere. It seemed to drift from a distant fog and slowly swell into reality.

He looked at Denny Benton.

The man asked: "You feeling okay?"

He shook his head. "I feel like hell, but that doesn't really matter. Nothing matters, right now."

He sat down on the hard cot that had been assigned to him. "I guess I'm just plain mentally tired!"

"First time in?

"You might say that."

"After a while you won't think nothin' about it. I spent some time once. After the first six months you get used to it; it won't seem so bloody bad."

"Thanks a lot!" Barry cursed bitterly, half aloud. "You're a *great* help!"

"Sorry."

There was a silence after that. For how long, Barry didn't know. It might have been seconds; minutes; or hours.

"Say, what happened to Blacky?" Benton asked, he was sitting opposite Barry on his own cot. He somehow looked quite at home in the cell. It almost seemed like his normal surroundings; as if he had been born to be in jail. "Where's Blacky?"

"Dead."

Shock showed on the man's face, The disbelief blanched every feature, making his nose seem like a milky white beak of some monstrous other-world creature. "You're kidding!"

"No. Dead. But good. Finished! That's one of the reasons they're holding me, now. They have Ann, too."

"Ann?"

"Cummings."

"Oh, his whore!"

That line made Barry want to smash the guy in the face. But it wasn't Benton's fault, really. He wasn't the one responsible for Ann having been Jenson's mistress; he had only said the truth. Anyway, he didn't have any way of knowing Barry's attachment to Ann. That was something that had just come out in the open. Nobody knew about it except Ann and himself. And Joan had known.

Joan.

The poor girl, That was a hurt, too. They had been pretty close. Too close for their own good. The relationship had been a strong and strange one; the kind that normally didn't develop; the kind that seemed slightly fantastic, now that he looked back at it.

Joan had been probably one of the most unselfish people he would ever know; or anybody had ever known. Their last days together had been hopeless ones, from her point of view. Yet, she had given of herself without any demands on

153

him. She had only wanted to help.

Yet, at the time, everything had seemed real and logical enough. It had seemed normal for Joan to act the way she did. Maybe because it had seemed her natural self; or real self showing through the hard outer shell she had placed up to the world.

To most, she had been nothing but a tramp and a lush. But he would rather know more tramps and lushes like her than some of the so-called decent people he had known in the past. A lot went religiously to church on Sundays for a spiritual bath and forgiveness for sins real and imagined; and then ran out eagerly the rest of the week to screw the world for any kind of profit they could steal into their greedy little eager hot, spiritually washed hands. The hypocrites were the real perverse criminals that lived normal, everyday lives, struggling to just simply survive the best they knew how. The truth of life was it could be hell to make it just through the next day. And that's where the churches of the world profited rich on society's desperate need for redemption. Perhaps that's what justified their existence, even if by some cruel fate it turned out there wasn't any God, no after-life, just this living hell on earth, born to die.

He hated to think that was possible. He would rather believe in some kind of afterlife, that a spiritual universe existed that would gather up souls that continued to live beyond this earthly existence.

For if death was truly the end, as it should be for the Blacky's of the world, then Joan was lost, gone forever. He would rather accept a fantasy that she now lived in some heavenly dimension. He had almost sensed the existence of such a spiritual universe when flying. But that, of course, had been imagination sparked by the ecstasy of floating high above the world in the very air itself, surrounded by fleecy clouds.

He would rather believe than disbelieve.

But seldom did he find it possible to believe in anything but the moment, the instant reality or some projected future which realistically suggested itself by events past and present.

He tried to be honest with himself.

154

Joan had never lied to herself about herself. She had been honest in that way; and how many people could he think of that were honest? It took guts to admit what you were to yourself; not making excuses. That was one thing she had had to her credit; among other things. And…

Killing Jenson.

That had been pretty far out. How many other people would have done the same thing? It couldn't have been really for just personal gain or revenge—for there had been little satisfaction for her in that direction.

He liked to think that maybe she had done it because of love; for him. She had done it to give him a chance at happiness with Ann. He liked thinking of the killing in that way. Maybe because it boosted his own ego; and maybe also because it made Joan ever bigger in his eyes. Bigger, period!

And worthy of some heavenly reward.

Maybe that was most of it. The fact that he liked the idea of a so-called tramp and lush turning out to he a little more noble than most people.

In fact, she certainly had washed away all her earthly sins in such an act.

Joan had given most. She had given not only herself, but her life for the man she had loved. What else could a person ask of another human being?

It was funny how a man could have an emotional attachment toward two women. Especially as different as were Joan and Ann.

It seemed incredible that Joan was even dead.

Gone. Finished. Over with. Just like that. Without any right to plead for her life; without any second chance. One moment living, the next dead.

God, let there be a God to bless her in some wonderful way.

Now, at least, because of Joan, he and Ann were at least getting a second chance. Regardless of where it was leading them. Ann and himself were alive and breathing and being given that golden opportunity of making a new life out of the old.

So much had happened so fast. His whole life had changed overnight. It had all started the moment he had come to Los Angeles. That had been the beginning point.

Now, he thought maybe it was for the best.

Before coming out West to do business with Blacky he had been happy enough, just drifting. Making money where and when he could. Nothing really illegal; just bordering a little along that shadowy line which stretched the law, but didn't break it. Then this last deal—making money by shipping whores from town to town.

It had all been easy and simple, before Blacky.

Women had just been women, then. No emotional attachments. A body to enjoy for the pleasure it could give. Not a real person with desperate needs. Take them to bed; and be done with it. Some had been close to the relationship which had built between Joan and himself; but they hadn't ended in quite the same way. A couple of romances; but nothing like he had gone through with Ann.

And yet they didn't really know all that much about the details of each other's lives. Still, the binding union was totally complete between them. The personal histories would be shared in bits and pieces as they rebuilt their lives together, as they shared existence, day by day, creating a blanket of living experiences to cover their total beings for life.

If they could escape their immediate trap.

A lovely fantasy that might never even get a chance to sprout wings.

Too many things too fast.

"Tell me what happened," Benton's voice interrupted his thoughts.

"Tell you what?" Barry asked, not realizing what the man was talking about.

"What happened to Blacky? How'd he get it? From the syndicate boys?"

Barry explained. Benton listened quietly, without comment. His expression didn't change once. He just listened, looking at Barry or the floor or the far wall. Their eyes never made contact, though.

Afterwards, Benton just smiled and said, "Well, guess you're really in deep, then. Damn shame!"

Damn shame!

That was an understatement if he had ever heard one.

156

What a laugh!

It was a universal laugh. Of course it was a damn shame. It was more than that. It was hell; and there was nothing that he could do about it.

Nothing at all! At least not right now.

"I hear we're to be shipped to L.A." Benton said, after a long silence.

"Los Angeles?"

"Yeah, The D.A. down there was the one who pulled the rug out from under us. He must have just missed you."

"So, now what happens?

"Seen your lawyer?"

Lawyer?

He had forgotten all about it. Maybe because he was in such a mental daze. Maybe because things had happened too fast to really plan or think things out. These first few hours he had just kept to the truth; no lawyer could honestly have advised him to do differently, because the truth was simple enough; Joan had killed Jensen and Jensen, Joan. It couldn't really be complicated or twisted out-of-shape. Joan had killed and been killed. Plenty of motives. The facts provable enough.

But a lawyer might be able to get them out on bail. That was a thought he hadn't given much attention to before. If Ann and himself could get out on bail it would make the days between the trial and now seem a lot easier to take; it would make them move faster, too.

Benton's voice slowly brought his attention back to the present. "...and that's the way I look at it. If we give out with a little information about the right guys, then maybe we might get off with a light sentence. I'm for making a deal with the D.A."

That was another idea. A good one. A damn good one! It might be a way out; out of a sentence. That's really why he and Ann had given themselves up. Their only hope lay in that direction. With the information Ann had and he could support and Benton was sure to add too, it seemed a strong bet that it would go damn good for them.

Maybe a light sentence.

Maybe off, Scot free.

It was the best chance they had, anyway.

His fists balled up tightly. He felt the blood pounding in his temples. His stomach knotted.

It was a damn shame. A dirty damn shame that they couldn't have their chance to happiness ... their freedom without all this blasted trouble!

But if there was a chance, he'd make it happen!

Chapter *NINETEEN*

In the last couple of weeks a lot had happened. It all seemed fantastic to him, now that he was looking back at those events and forward to the trial which was to take place the next morning. It wasn't exactly a trial, just a hearing before the judge to decide what was to be done about the case against him.

Tomorrow his fate would be decided and there was nothing he would be able to do after that except fight like hell for his freedom.

The law had decided to move fast. It seemed when it made up its mind about something it could go at a head-spinning rate of speed. The D.A., Mr. Wilson, had been ready and anxious to push this case to the bitter end, before a defense could be built by the syndicate lawyers. He was making his major move not at Barry, but at the real target; the people responsible for the rackets which Blacky Jensen had been in.

As far as Wilson was concerned, Barry was just a means to an end. He had already dropped any and all charges which connected him with the killing of Jenson and Joan. That had been easy enough to get him to do. *There wasn't any case.*

Luckily, for him, the D.A.'s office had been given orders to be lenient on those who were willing to give information which might lead to the real ring-leaders of the call-girl racket. It was an election year and if the rackets could be, at least momentarily, closed down in California, it would look good for the party in office. A simple matter of politics.

The action had started the moment they had arrived in Los Angeles. Barry had called a lawyer whose name Benton had given him. At first he had been hesitant about anybody which this man might recommend; but as it turned out, Mr.

159

Landing was perfect for the case.

"He's not what you think," Benton had explained, heatedly. "Sure, when he was a kid he got himself into trouble with the law, was sent to reform school and came out looking good. He's what you might call a reform lawyer. He won't touch anything that's not up-and-up. Touchy as hell about it. But he'd be perfect. He likes to deal with people like you, who just got out of line once, like you tell me you did, and guys like me who are willing to turn in states evidence. The D.A. will play ball with Landing, too. Believe me, *this is our only man!*"

He had talked to Landing by long-distance phone. The man sounded honest. He sounded like a livewire, too.

"Tell me what the deal is," Landing had said to him. "From what you've said, you're willing to play ball. That's not enough. I want to know something about you. Check up on your past record."

The man wanted to know everything about his past. And Barry told him everything. Enough so that the man could do all the checking he wanted. One thing that Barry wanted more than anything now was to get completely clear of his past. Make a clean break and start over. His whole trouble had been that there had never been any focal point on which he could place all his attention.

Now he had Ann. That would he enough for him to work his brains out to build a happy life and future for them. The only way he could do that was clear the whole thing up—completely; holding nothing back.

He would do anything Landing wanted him to do.

When he arrived in Los Angeles he was met by two men—the D.A. and a lawyer.

His attorney was large. Big. Clean-faced. Penetrating eyes which were deep-set and intelligent-looking.

"Glad to meet you, Davis," Landing greeted, as they stepped into the squad car which the D.A. had come in. "This is Mr. Wilson, the man we have to fight in court." He laughed at the last remark. From the way he acted, a person would have thought the whole thing was some kind of picnic.

Maybe to the legal men it was!

160

Justice was seldom a reality in the court system. It was winner takes all, and the loser, guilty or not, got caught in the machinery that choked in tightly with crushing power.

To Barry it was deadly serious. Too deadly serious to be light and witty about.

Nothing beyond remarks about the weather and the smog were exchanged until they arrived at the D.A.'s office. Once the doors had been closed behind them everything became serious.

"Sit down, Mr. Davis," Wilson said, stepping around a large desk and following his own advice. "Make yourself comfortable."

A Sunday picnic! Crap!

He sat. Landing sat next to him.

His attorney spoke next. "Since I talked to you the other day I've done a little investigating. I don't like getting involved with the wrong kind of people; a person in my business is better making sure that he can believe in the client. What I want you to understand is that if I go to bat for you, you have to play along with me; do what I tell you and don't try being smart. Or smart-assed!"

This he didn't get. From what he thought he knew about the relationship between a lawyer and client, it was the client who made the rules, and then the attorney went along with them.

"From what I've seen of your record," Landing continued, leaning forward and looking directly into his eyes, "it would seem that you're the kind of man I like to do business with.

There was a silence after that.

Mr. Wilson broke it.

"This is a little odd way of handling things, but Mr. Landing has a peculiar way of doing business. You have to understand a little about his past." The D.A. leaned hack in his seat, slowly took a puff of his cigarette and then after breathing out the smoke, continued. "You see, most lawyers don't take the time to become known for helping crooks and law-breakers to reform. Landing here does just this. He's dedicated his life's work in that direction. He has quite a reputation among criminals; they look him up any time they get into trouble."

"And I don't take all their cases, I might add," Landing interjected.

"A man in his position has to be careful, because he can get a *bad* reputation. Many men do have this kind of reputation. You're lucky that he's even considering handling you."

"I thought that he had already—"

"No, Mr. Davis. Far from it." Landing's voice was soft, but the force behind the words left Barry slightly dazed.

"Then why are we here?"

"Simple, Mr. Davis," Wilson said, smiling slightly. "To see just how we will handle your case."

"I don't get it!" Barry exclaimed. "You act as if you work as a team—or something! Why the hell—"

"Take it easy," Landing quickly cut in, patting him on the shoulder. "Wilson has slightly over-simplified the matter—*as he normally does!* It's all much more complicated than this." There was silence after that. Then his attorney continued.

"You have to understand that though I work as the defense for a variety of known crooks, I also work hand-in-hand with the D.A."

That was a blow out of left field! What the hell had Benton gotten him into?

"I don't get it at all, Landing."

"Well, look at it this way. My major concern is reforming. I'm more interested in what a client will do and be *after* his case has been won or lost; in fact, in either event!"

"In other words," Barry snapped, feeling slightly nauseated, "you don't worry about winning or losing; only in…"

"In helping people get back on the right track. *Regardless of how it is done.* I don't believe that it is necessary to put a person in jail in order to straighten him out. In some cases this is the only way to solve their problem. In my *own* this turned out to be the truth. I'm, to be honest about it, am interesting in justice for all—and society itself, too. The bad guys go in jail; the good guys get a break! But in your case, I believe that other measures are in line."

And that means exactly what?

"It so happens that Wilson here goes along with this

162

theory, to some degree. Also, the fact that he has other interests in this case."

"In other words, Mr. Davis," the D.A. added, "you are just small fish. I want the big whales. If you can in any way help me tag them I can be a great help to you."

There was a silence.

Barry didn't know what to say. There wasn't anything *to* say. The fact was that he didn't really know who the big shots were. He had no idea. He was just a smaller fish among mini-fish who knew more than he did.

Taking a big breath he nervously leaned forward, looking Wilson straight in the eyes. "I want to help all I can. Believe me in that. This is the first time I've really stepped this far into the red...so to speak. And I want out. As I said in my statement, I turned myself in, freely and without any attempts to lie my way out. We might have tried to make a break for Mexico with the plane. Drop the bodies out in the desert where they would never be found. But I decided it wouldn't do any good to be running all my life. That's all I've been doing for the past years. Always been taking the easy way out. Well, I decided not to do this, this time."

Wilson shook his head knowingly. "We realize all this. That's why you are here. Both Landing and our office have done a complete checkup in this matter. Your past is completely known to us. The major part, that is. Your war record is good! You don't have any police record in *any* state. This is, for all legal purposes, your first offense. To be honest, we don't give a damn about you."

"But you don't understand!" Barry objected. "It's not my unwillingness to help. It's just my lack of ability."

The silence was deafening.

"I don't get it!" Wilson exclaimed.

"Well, put it this way. I was only in on two jobs. The pay was a thousand dollars a trip, plus expenses—"

"You're kidding!" the D.A. exploded, his breath shooting out of him like a rocket. "For taking up broads?"

Landing laughed. "I'm in the wrong racket."

"I don't know what to tell you," Barry continued. "I guess they planned to get me in deeper. That's what Ann told me."

"Ann? Who?" Landing asked.

"That would be Miss Cummings," Wilson quickly explained. "Continue."

"Well, both Ann and Joan knew a lot about the deal. Ann said that if I didn't get out fast, then it would be too late. This flight to Boise was my finish. Jenson didn't know it, but I was going to quit them. But other complications entered in. You don't know how close I came to killing Jenson...but that's another story...I made two thousand dollars for the two jobs. This I'm turning over to Landing; or your office. I don't give a damn what happens to it. I just don't want anything to do with it."

"We know all about this. You told Landing, and Landing told us." Wilson was getting impatient. "Get on with the point."

"The point is that I wasn't told anything. They just gave me instructions when to take the girls and where to drop them. That was my job. Nothing else."

"I might add," Landing interjected, looking at Wilson, "I could have advised Davis, here, to keep silent about this matter *in court*. He might have been able to prove *in court* that he never knew the real reasons for his flights. We might have lost the point but it would have been a good fight. It was his idea to tell the whole thing.

"Oh, come off it. I know all this!"

"Well, then," Barry continued, "then you must know that I just don't have any information to trade. Ann does. And so does Benton. But, as for me, I don't have anything to sell!"

"Don't be so sure about that, Mr. Davis," Wilson pointed out, tapping a finger on the edge of the desk. "You'd be surprised how much you know. Little things which might not seem important to you, but to the prosecution it would help a lot of help. All I'm concerned with today is making you see this point and also find out just how cooperative you plan on being. Landing said you had told him you were willing to give out with all the information you had. Tell what you know in court; and let *us* decide just how important it is. As for the case against you of taking women over the state line for immoral purposes, I think that the law can find some

164

loophole to help you out. After all, it's not the strict en-
forcement of the law that we are concerned with in your case
as much as justice; and, as Mr. Landing might put it, bringing an end to the career of a possible future professional
criminal, *before* it is too late to stop it, without stronger legal
means—it is far better to reform *outside* of prison than con-
taminate a possible good citizen by penning him imp with a
lot of professional convicts."

"Nicely quoted," Landing laughed, good-naturedly.

"*We* aren't promising you anything. No deals," the D.A.
continued. "just saying that both of us feel that in cases like
yours it is better to attempt reform—or a second chance, if
you like that term—than taking a chance of doing more
damage by putting you away for several years. But it *is* up to
the judge. Not me. I'm after the big fish. You're a possible
road. If you help us as best you can I'll do what I am able to
help you."

"Davis," Landing said, turning toward Barry, "believe
me, you're in a tight spot. Even with Wilson's help here, and
all the angels on your shoulder, it might take an act of Cod
itself to keep you out of jail. Two years at least. But your
chances are much better by playing along."

Barry didn't really see what the point was. They had already known that he was willing to play ball; tell all; sing
like a bird. This seemed like just so much double-talk.

"Okay, tell me in simple terms, so that even a child can
understand. Exactly what is this all about?" Barry asked,
leaning forward, wetting his lips and trying to hold down the
hard knot of fear that kept telling him that no matter what he
did he would be in jail for a long, long time. "Exactly why
have you taken all this time and energy to ask me to do
something which I already promised I'd do."

"Simple," Wilson said, smiling warmly for the first
time. "We wanted to know, first hand, what kind of man you
were. This Benton fellow we know well enough, from his
record. You and Ann Cummings are something different.
You see, there aren't really any charges against Miss Cummings. She could get out of here without saying a word. To
put it bluntly: she could easily lie herself blue in the fact and
there would be no real way of proving her story false. Mis-

tresses many times don't know what's going on; and if they do it's always possible that the law won't play hardball unless they have to. Fact of the matter is: deals can be made! This is the case with the Cummings girl."

Landing took it up from there. "You see, Davis, without Miss Cummings' testimony you *don't* have as much in your favor. In a word: she's your case!

"I realize that this all must seem pretty odd. But. again, I want to point out that the D.A. and myself are more interested in being fair. And Wilson is interested only in the ringleaders."

Barry didn't like it. He didn't like getting out or even getting a chance of a lesser sentence on the possibility that Ann might be caught up in a nightmare trap. And that's the way it looked. The thing they seemed to be getting at. She was his case. What would happen to her?

It was quite a shock to see how cold-bloodedly these two men could plan behind the scenes to work so closely together.

"You see, Mr. Davis," Wilson announced, standing and walking around his desk, "Miss Cummings might fairly well be our key witness. We figure that if you were the kind of guy we hoped you'd turn out to be, we'd get your help."

They were guessing that keeping him in a state of danger, then Ann might play right into their hands. They knew a lot more than he wished they did. They at the very least understood that a woman in love would do anything to protect her man.

But her man would do anything to protect her, too.

Barry was too dazed to be mad. He couldn't even think. Just a red haze was clouding his vision. A real haze of mental fury and confusion.

He was a zombie when he was led from the D.A.'s office. He didn't come out of it until he was locked behind bars.

That's when he knew he had to turn down the D.A.'s offer. That's when he cleared the shocked numbness away from his mind and felt the first stabbing pains of disgusted madness.

The damn bastards! His mind screamed over and over.

The dirty little slobs!

But then the fury ebbed away. And it was replaced with confusion.

He couldn't have Ann endanger herself in order to give him a chance for freedom. He couldn't let her.

Yet...

Yet, what else was there to do?

Five to ten years in jail? He didn't know what it might be. If the D.A. decided to push him into a hole there was no knowing how far in the man could shove. No doubt he could think up plenty of charges against Barry. *Now that he thought about it.*

A thousand dollars a job to just fly call-girls around? That would look pretty silly in court. Nobody would believe him that this was all he was being paid for. The D.A. could think of a hundred possible crimes he *might* be guilty of. And from that man's logic, if you ain't guilty of this crime you probably are of some other equally horrid crime—or will be in the future.

And the horrible truth was he might just be innocently guilty of them!

Chapter *TWENTY*

Barry's attorney, Landing, visited his cell several times during the next few days. The relationship was an odd one. But one thing Barry did learn was that Landing was his best, if not only, chance of getting out of the trouble—if there were any chance at all for him.

The first visit was the most difficult. After that they were on a better relationship with each other. Up to this point Barry had been living in a world of confusion. The first meeting with Landing had left him with mixed reactions. It didn't seem like the man was working for the right side. From the way the conversation had drifted it seemed that the D.A. and Landing worked hand-in-hand. Which looked to him more than just "odd."

You expect your lawyer to be working only for you; and not with the D.A.'s office.

The moment Barry heard that Landing was on his way to see him, he began feeling a nervous drag on his insides.

He lighted a cigarette.

Puffed nervously.

Landing arrived. The cell door opened and he walked in.

"How are you?" the man asked, extending his hand. "I'm sorry that it took so long before I got down here to see you. I've been continuing my investigation of you. The most important thing, from my viewpoint, is getting to know all there is about you. This will be necessary if we are to get you out free. I understand that Judge Patterson is going to be hearing the case. He's a hard, by-the-book man." Landing sat on the edge of the lone cot.

Barry remained standing.

"Look," Barry said, before the other man had a chance to continue, "I want to get a few things settled. I've had

168

some time to think a bit since I saw you last. I don't know if I...well—"

"Shoot."

Several days had passed since he had seen the man in the D.A.'s office, and he had had plenty of time to wonder if Landing was the right lawyer for him. But it was hard to just come right out and say it.

"I want some simple facts." Barry started pacing the floor. The cigarette in his hand was already half finished and he was dragging on it furiously. "One is: just how do you stand *in* the case? Are you for me? Or are you working for Wilson?"

The other laughed. "In court things will be different. You'll find me far from friendly with Wilson, if necessary. But I don't think it will be. But don't worry. I'll fight for you in every way possible."

"Then what about the other day?"

"Like we said, that was just to see how to handle you. Wilson could take the charges to court with a jury right now. Or he can just go before a judge for a hearing. He wants an informal hearing, after having talked to you. The reason for our talk was to see if he could make that decision. See if you were willing to help out; and if it was worth our while to attempt to set aside the charges against you for the chance of getting the important men.

"You see, in a case like this, I'm even more interested in seeing the guilty people in jail that the D.A.'s office. I believe strongly in getting the right people behind bars. But I also believe that there is no sense in putting people like yourself into a position of getting in deeper than you already are—if you are really honest about you wanting to start out new.

"Remember, the whole idea of reform is to help people who made a mistake get a new chance. Jail is to punish lawbreakers. But what are the reasons for punishment? *To make the man or woman not want to make the same mistake twice!* You spank a child's hand so that it won't be bad again. An adult who breaks the law is put in jail or fined so that they won't break the law again. Or so it is hoped.

"In your case, as a result of your actions, I have every

reason to believe that you've already seen your mistake and don't want to get into such a jam again ..."

"That's for damn sure!" Barry meant it.

"Still, that wouldn't be enough. In any case, I think that the information that you and Miss Cummings and Benton can give the D.A. is much more important than putting you behind bars. I don't believe it's necessary to punish a person who already has changed. Your act of turning yourself in willingly proved that well enough. It should, anyway, to any judge or jury.

"To be truthful, if this weren't the case, I wouldn't have taken you on."

But that just repeated what he had heard already.

It told him nothing really new.

"Okay, taking it from there. What's this bit about Ann Cummings?" Barry paused in front of the other man. "I couldn't say some of the things I wanted to, the other afternoon, but I don't like this idea of her being used. Pushed into a corner. I don't like my being charged to satisfy some need to press the woman I love into a position where she could be in danger—"

"I know. That's why I'm here, now."

"Then, what about Ann?"

"She's being held until after the hearing; as you are."

"I take it, then, that you plan on her talking."

"She already said that she would. Has made a statement to that effect."

"Then it was all the time out of my hands..."

"In a matter of speaking, yes."

Barry didn't like that. But there wasn't anything he could do about it, now. Somehow he felt relieved. And because of that relief, he felt something else.

Guilt!

Landing stood up, to accent his next words. "I don't think you realize exactly the full extent of this whole thing. It is more than just Jensen. He was bad enough. We have conclusive information of his direct connection with smuggling, marketing and handling of narcotics. Two years ago the D.A.'s office, here in Los Angeles, tried to prove that he was connected with the actual killing of a private investigator.

170

They couldn't do it. *He was guilty!* They knew it then; and only now are they able to prove it. Jensen also had a nice little business on the side. Taking care of girls in trouble. The operations were a couple of times botched up so. In fact, too many times botched! And so badly that it was necessary for him to get rid of the girls. In one case dumping her body in the ocean. She was never found. He didn't seem to mind in the least. I knew about it then, but there was nothing that I, or anyone, could do. No proof. Jenson had come to me to get legal help; I naturally refused. His was the kind of case I won't ever handle. I didn't want any part of it. Then or now."

Landing paused for a moment. His voice in the last few sentences had raised and his face distorted to red. His hands were slightly shaking. *"That little bastard!"*

Then he gained control after a long moment of silence. "If it weren't for your good past record, I wouldn't have touched you, either—and Benton's being handled only because of the information he has given the authorities which will help the two of you—Miss Cummings and yourself."

"Okay, all I want to know then, is: what's going to happen? What are my chances? In other words, what can I expect?"

"Well, there will be a hearing before Judge Patterson in a couple of days. Wilson wants to get on with it. If he can give the F.B.I. information that will lead to the arrest and jailing of the men responsible for Jenson's operations here in Los Angeles, it will not only help his career and assure his reelection, but also help quite a few other people. That's one of our major breaks in the ease; along with the fact that Wilson doesn't really *have* any case against you."

That was a jolt out of left field.

"What do you mean?"

"Well, the murder charge doesn't count. That has been technically dropped, but the judge will hear the case anyway."

"I thought…"

"That's only a matter of routine. Wilson wants to make it official. Once that point has *been* established, it will help you out, actually. I'm for this. In fact, I made it a point to ask Wilson to bring it up. Once it has been legally ruled on it can

171

never be brought up again. It will also establish your motives and actions after the killings. It will tell a lot of background information which will be necessary to sway Judge Patterson to look lightly on the other charge."

"Okay, then what?"

"Then we present the case on the Mann Act charge. Your illegal transportation of women across the state line for immoral purposes. That's a Federal offense. It can't be dropped. It has to be seen through.

"Basically, though, the facts are that you weren't caught in the actual act of transporting women. There isn't any hard evidence to that fact. Only your connection with Jenson, plus other facts which imply it, and your own statements. The only real evidence the D.A. has is that you mentioned the activities. But no recordings were being made, and it would just be his word against yours. Of course, lying on the stand is a serious matter; but just the possibility that you *could* get away with it is enough to make Wilson willing to forget that statement, if it serves justice better by doing so.

"I might have seemed buddy-buddy with him while we were all together the other day, but in actual fact we'd sorted through these realities before that meeting. In other words, by working *with* Wilson we are getting every break that he can give us. Mainly, because we all feel that it would do little good putting you behind bars.

"That doesn't mean you'll get off free—that will depend on the judge. It only means that Wilson and myself are going to do everything we can to convince the judge to set you free. Or at the very least a very light sentence."

For the first time Barry saw the possibility of light; just a little glimmering of light; but it was better than nothing.

Maybe his chances of that second chance were beginning to show signs of materializing into reality, after all.

"In a couple of days the hearing will be brought up before Patterson. That's when it will be decided if we have an ironclad case against the real people responsible; and if we can get the charges dropped against you."

After that the conversation of that visit and all the later ones covered Barry's past. Landing wanted to know everything about him. From the moment he was born. Where he lived. The people he knew. The things he had done. What his future plans were.

That last question was simple. Marry Ann Cummings.

Landing laughed at that. "Because that's exactly what Miss Cummings told me."

He wanted to know anything and everything that might make a tough judge soften a little.

It all seemed like a long, endless, hellish nightmare. A devil's dream which seemed to never end. Day and night the small cell became his world. Landing's visits being his only contact with the outside.

He tried to get permission to see Ann, but Landing advised against it. "As long as you are kept apart, there can be no chance of anybody saying that you collaborated in your stories. There is less chance of anybody claiming that you are lying."

The man no doubt had his other reasons. Legal. It really didn't matter, and Barry didn't push it. He might have even felt worse seeing Ann. For, in the cell, it was possible to almost act as if this *were* all just a bad nightmare. It was easier to live through it because he could refuse to think about anything that might make it seem more hellish.

Think about Ann. And that was hell. Because he wanted to take her in his arms. Hold her lips against his. Feel the warmth of her kisses. Her arms clutching tightly; the pressure of that delicate form against his.

He wanted to feel, touch, and smell and experience her nearness.

But he refused to let his mind think about her. He did everything possible to put her out of his thoughts. And, somehow, he managed to do a fair job of it.

The fact that he survived those few days was only because he managed to think of other things outside of her and himself. Thought of her brought dreams and plans for the future; and he wasn't so sure that he had any beyond the bleak walls of a prison cell.

Chapter *TWENTY-ONE*

The trial. Hearing. Whatever they wanted to call it; Barry called it Hell!

The night before he hadn't slept well. Thinking about what might happen in court was enough to keep sleep always just a little away from him. Thought that Judge Patterson was a person who didn't instantly buy the same liberal ideas that Landing and Wilson held, wasn't much of a help either.

But there was one compensation: Ann was there. He was surprised how much he had missed her. Sure, he was aware of the fact she was the most important thing in his life; but when she walked into the Judge's chambers and sat down next to him, all the emotions he had been holding back for so many days, welled up in him, making his head lightly dizzy.

They had known each other for so little time; yet she was more important to him than life itself. And life without her would not be worth living.

They had gone through so much together.

In so short a time.

They still had the biggest battle ahead. If they managed to make it through this last struggle, they would have each other and freedom.

At least, that was better than they could have hoped before Jenson was killed.

It was more than Joan had gotten.

As Ann sat down next to him, he turned, smiled and reached out a hand and touched her. The contact was still electric.

God, how he loved her!

She smiled back. The corners of her full lips moved upwards. It was a tired action. Her whole face seemed slightly drawn looking. Each feature thinner. But she was still beautiful.

"How're things?" he asked.

"Okay, I guess," was all she had said; that was the extent of their verbal conversation.

Throughout the morning they exchanged frightened looks, but said nothing.

Yet just having her there helped. Moral courage. It gave him something else to think about, outside of what was going on around him.

Everybody was told to stand as the judge entered. Then they seated themselves.

Barry wasn't really aware of what was going on for the first few minutes. His mind was thinking over the past couple of weeks. The loneliness of the last few days. The anxious waiting, the importance of what was taking place right then.

His eyes looked up at the judge. The man was stony-faced. His features chiseled and unmoving. Judge Ralph P. Patterson. A man in his late fifties. His expression heavy and set. Hard gray eyes glanced over in Ann's direction for a moment and then looked at Barry. Not a hint showed as to the way the man felt toward them.

"Your Honor," the D.A. was saying, standing quietly in front of the judge. "Because of the circumstances of this case, and the two people involved, I ask your permission to proceed in an informal manner and that you consider my recommendation to be lenient." He paused for a moment, and then continued. "The two counts on which Mr. Davis is being charged with are questionable and I believe that it would be doing justice in his case to waive them."

"I've looked at the charges," Judge Patterson said in a stiff, low voice. "At this point I don't see any reason for your recommendation.

"As for your motion that we keep this informal, I see no reason why that can't be done. That is the basic reason for this hearing in my private chambers, instead of a court room."

"Thank you, your honor."

"However, I will, under these circumstances, still demand that the case on both counts be reviewed here and now.

175

After which I'll make a decision as to what should happen then. If I see reason of any kind to continue matters to a full court trial, it shall be so. We will see..."

The voice faded out. Barry wasn't paying any attention anymore. He was too tired to pay close attention. As far as the judge and Wilson and Landing were concerned, Barry and Ann were nothing but names. Not personalities. Not living, breathing human beings, whose lives could be crushed by just one word.

Regardless of the informal arrangements, this was a court of law and the men who were in charge were the only ones who really seemed to count. In their hands, and nobody else's, Barry and Ann's fate was to be decided.

Slowly, bit by bit, the story of how Jenson and Joan were killed was told. The Judge just sat quietly, listening. Not moving. It was covered from beginning to end. No witnesses were called in, because, basically, this was just a matter of reviewing the facts and seeing exactly what could or couldn't be made of them. A lot of unread reports were included from medical professionals and police files. And all the statements Ann and Barry had made. This was for the record; they were all quietly accepted by the judge who simply nodded when they were mentioned. Apparently he had read all of them previously. In fact there was a feeling that everything had been decided previous to this hearing. It seemed as if this were just some kind of perverse act, leading up to a horrid life shattering sentence.

All Wilson was concerned with, first, as Landing had told him the day before, was to make it official that no crime had been committed by Barry or Ann in the case of the death of Joan or Jenson.

"It would seem," Judge Patterson said, not without humor, when Wilson had finished, "That you are working more for the defense than otherwise."

Was that a statement simply for the "record"?

"That is not really the case here, your Honor. What I am interested in, as is Mr. Landing, is simply looking at the facts honestly. The thing, I believe, is to determine if there is really any solid charge which would hold up against Mr. Davis and Miss Cummings on the deaths of Joan Verril and

176

Hubert 'Blacky' Jenson."

"I believe that you've covered that matter quite well," Judge Patterson said, leaning forward.

"Then, for the record's sake, can we officially drop this charge?"

"I believe so. There doesn't seem to be evidence of any kind to not support the fact that they had nothing to do with the two deaths involved. In actual fact they are witnesses to what actually took place. And the medical facts seem to support that. As you so well pointed out, they landed at Boise of their own free will. The fingerprints on the gun and the way the bodies were found seemed to indicate that their original statements, which you quoted, were quite true. I rule that the charges be dropped. That's official. On the record. Happy?"

"Now," Wilson said, stepping back to his own desk and picking up some papers. "We have a unique situation here. Any charge of Mr. Davis having actually transported or was connected to, or involved with, the transportation of women across the state border for immoral purposes would be a difficult thing to prove compulsively. Only a statement made to me privately could in any way support or—"

"I object, your honor," Landing spoke up for the first time. "What Mr. Wilson might or might not have heard cannot have any bearing on the case. It would only be his word against my client's."

Wilson quickly explained "I was about to say that."

"Then continue, Judge Patterson ordered.

"The point I wish to make here is that, while it might be difficult to prove, it is still a possibility. But, in view of the other circumstances of the case, which I am sure you have studied in full, I recommend that the charges be dropped for lack of evidence."

It seemed impossible to Barry the way things had happened. From his own viewpoint he had been guilty, but he didn't actually think that the law could be so flexible as to overlook that guilt. Even the slightest.

After Wilson had made his motion that the case against him he dropped, Judge Patterson turned in his direction.

"Will the defendant rise?"

Barry did so.

"I want it understood that this court is not in the habit of doing anything but following the letter of the law to the end." The Judge coughed, looked down at the papers on his desk and then back up to Barry. "I imagine that you realize the seriousness of what you got yourself into. I also realize that you are guilty as hell and back!"

There was a pause at that point.

"I might add!" he continued, after a long moment, "I *have* studied the facts very carefully. Actually, this hearing has only been a legal means of putting everything on the record. Both Mr. Wilson and Mr. Landing have presented their cases in writing, which included case histories of both of you, and also all the statements which were made. As has been indicated by our…statements this morning."

Another silence.

"Like I said, you *are* guilty of this last charge. It's a Federal offense. Normally a long jail sentence is the punishment. And from the legal sense, you deserve just that.

"But, because of Wilson's and Landing's personal recommendations and each of their past records in judging correctly in such matters, I have been forced, in all honesty, to look at this whole affair in a different light.

"The jails are already filled with far too many people. But that wouldn't decide me, in either case. The fact remains, regardless of all else, that the evidence against you is not conclusive enough to bring you to trial. A jury would, no doubt, be forced to turn in a verdict of not guilty, or at best, guilty, but with a recommendation to be lenient,

"I believe that we can save the taxpayers' money and everybody a lot of time and effort. Like Mr. Wilson pointed out today, the important thing is to deal out *proper* justice; and in this case I believe that the following should he done:

"The case to be shelved to a future date; *indefinite*. Only to *be* brought forth in the event that you are ever brought before any court of law for *any* reason in the future which might involve such a felony charge. Or if you refuse to give the promised evidence in the trials of the people responsible for the crimes in which you have been involved.

"That you be put on bail for the $2,000 which Mr. Landing said you didn't know what to do with and, beyond that

—Case dismissed!"

* * * * * * *

Six months had passed since that first "trail" and judgment.

Those months had brought a mixture of happiness and hell. But now the hell was all over. The D.A.'s office happily satisfied with their convictions of the head men who had been behind Jenson's operations in Los Angeles.

But Barry and Ann had come out with their second chance. And that's all that really counted to Barry.

When Judge Patterson had announced those last words, Barry had stood silently for a long time, frozen with happiness. It seemed too good to be true. It seemed too good to be true. It seemed impossible.

Yet, there it was.

They were free. Free to start over. A life together. A future which could be built and shaped out of the lessons of the past.

In the months that had followed, Barry had started working for an airline company which Mr. Landing had recommended to him. Those first months had been difficult ones. But now they were over.

Barry impatiently stamped out his cigarette, pushing the little white cylinder into the ground.

Where was Ann?

She was late, as usual!

Then he saw her in a white summer dress, strolling down the walkway. She smiled as she stepped up to him.

"And how's my husband today?" she asked, kissing him gently on the cheek.

"That's what I call a silly question!" he laughed, holding her tightly to him. "After a long twenty-four-hour haul, and you want to know just how I am!"

"I'm sorry about being late, but I had to stop by—"

"You're always late picking me up. You know what I'm going to do one of these days. Either take that car away from you and leave it here at the airport for me, or get another one." He laughed happily as they walked to the parking lot and stopped in front of a new blue convertible.

Things had changed a lot for them. They had also brought a lot of new things into their lives. Like this car. A house they were tied down to for the next twenty years or so. But it was all theirs and the bank's.

"About that new car," Ann said, as she slid into the seat next to him. "I don't think you'll be able to afford it for some time.

"Then you'll have to just learn to be on time picking me up. These flights are!"

"But, you don't understand!"

"What?"

"Where I was today."

"So, where were you?" He directed the car onto the highway.

"The reason I was late." Her voice sounded strangely different. Happier than he had heard her ever sound before, A certain hidden glow to it.

"Okay, I'll bite. Why were you late?"

"I was at the doctor's today."

His heart almost stopped.

"What's wrong?" he said, afraid that something might be.

"Don't be so worried. The doctor said that I'm going to have a baby!"

He didn't hear the rest, then. His heart stopped beating completely—for a second, Then it pounded faster. So fast that it seemed the beats ran together.

Somehow he managed to keep the car on the road.

Yes sir! his mind screamed, happily, *things were really picking up.*

A future filled with real hot cargo—the hottest there was: a wife, home, kids, and happiness.

What else could a slob like him wish for?